Free Space:
The Real Life Story of a
Bingo Queen

Jeremy Vaeni

Kynegion House

Free Space   Jeremy Vaeni

Kynegion House

Cover Design: Kynegion House
Printed In USA

Special Thanks

Mary Vaeni for editing, input, and genuine concern that I would isolate my audience with potty-mouth humor. How do you explain to your mom that it's your specialty?

The real Bingo Palace without which none of this would have been possible.

Free Space   Jeremy Vaeni

This book is dedicated to everyone reading who stuck with me from the beginning. I know you didn't sign up for comedy fiction when you got to know me as an experiencer of high strangeness or... well... that guy who claimed to have become God that one day there. Although reading this back to myself I'm thinking maybe you did.

This series is equally dedicated to everyone discovering my writing now. Good for you!

Free Space   Jeremy Vaeni

WELCOME TO THE

B-MOVIES IN A BOOK SERIES

Back in the day, whatever day that was, a B-movie meant the low-budget commercial flick that accompanied the main attraction in a double feature. Somewhere along the way to today, whatever day this is, *B-movie* came to mean what I affectionately call a *shit film*.

Shit films come in all scents but most notably horror, science fiction, and screwball comedy. But not the good kind of screwball comedy with the potty-mouthed stars you know and love; usually the ones with the bare-chested 30-something actresses playing high school or college girls and their cliched male counterparts who have the emotional depth of a spermatozoon.

When done right a shit film can be every bit as good as the big budget A-lister it wishes it were. In fact, better. Better because its aim is lower, audience expectation lower still, and so with the right script and the right cameo from a failed decent actor of yesteryear believing this to be his/her comeback roll, it could end up a satisfying work of genius that for whatever reason Hollywood giants passed on or never glanced at in the first place.

I love shit films. Though I grew up on George Lucas and John Hughes, it wasn't until I popped *Evil Dead 2* into my VCR that I knew I had to be a movie director. What Sam Raimi did with a camera, the physical brilliance of star Bruce Campbell, and a rainbow of gory liquids, woke me up to the artistry that can be squeezed from a small budget. It doesn't have to be about lavish special effects or Oscar-caliber performances. Just a man, a camera, and a zoom lens.

At least that's the way it felt when I first watched it back in high school. The budget was about $3.5 million. I'm sure there was more than one camera and maybe even a dolly shot or two.

Nevertheless, *Evil Dead 2* got my creative juices flowing for what it represented: accessibility. I thought, 'I can do this.'

I figured if I could take the framework of a B-film, with the power of its low expectations, and write A-film dialogue, I could have a smash hit on my hands. I could rule the B-movie world. I could achieve the laziest dream of all:

becoming a millionaire from half-assing my art in an already half-assed art form, which would, by the sheer brilliance of me, make it full-assed.

Then I grew up and said fuck it. Let's move to Hawaii and forget about all that instead. If you're going to half-ass your passion, half-ass it all the way. No-ass it. Just live.

Now I'm here living in Hawaii, no-assing my way through life. But I've accumulated a drawer full of screenplays and fleshed-out ideas from the time when I dreamed slightly bigger. And I'm thinking it would be a shame to let these writings go to waste simply because I've lost my ambition to make a name for myself as the greatest director you never heard of. Shit, why can't I be the greatest writer you never heard of? These things are already written! Don't be a fool! Publish them!

I exclaim things a lot in my head. You'd be surprised. And surprised at the feedback. I digress....

The B-Movies In A Book Series is a labor of love, but make no mistake: it *is* a labor. There is no no-assing it the way I'd hoped, because the same want for a challenge I found in make A-calibre B-movies has resurfaced in creating their novelizations.

This series will not be one of sequels but of building a singular universe out of incredibly disparate parts. Every book will be connected—sometimes blatantly, sometimes vaguely or abstractly. But you won't miss anything by skipping the ones that are not in the genre you enjoy. So wait it out if you must. I'll eventually write a book that's for you. Hopefully, the one you're reading right now.

Free Space: The Real Life Story of a Bingo Queen is not the first screenplay I ever wrote, but it is the most difficult to translate into a book. This is because it is a mock documentary.

When was the last time you read a mock documentary? Never, is when.

Making this a reality was a serious challenge. And a fun one. I wanted to start off with my best work and my most intricately designed book to give myself something to try to top when I write the next in the series. *Free Space* is arguably the least B of all my screenplays (perhaps more indie than B, like *Waiting For Guffman*), but it best encapsulates the movie in a book feel due to it being a screenplay/prose hybrid. I doubt I'll do that with the others but here it's practically a necessity.

However, I can also put a check in the lazy column because this book ties into my first published work of (shockingly) nonfiction, *I Know Why The Aliens Don't Land!* (2003). The universe-building starts here and I didn't have to lift a mental finger for the idea to transcend this series into unrelated works, making me look like a genius. In my head. Where I exclaim things and receive feedback.

Digress? Yeah, let's do that again....

Readers of *I Know Why* already know the backstory to *Free Space* and are familiar with its lead. I won't retread it here except to say that although this is a work of fiction, much of the dialogue isn't as fake as I'd like it to be. It's amazing what you overhear and what people share with you directly when you're a stranger in a small town bingo palace. Or take a stripper to breakfast at four in the morning.

Yeah. I'm much better off writing from my bunker in Hawaii than trying to break through the front doors of the back lot of Hollywood. I was never one for hookers and blow. Or work.

On to the coming attraction!

COMING SOON

TO A BOOK NEAR YOU

B-Movies In A Book Series Presents....

"It's still real to me. . .."

In Association with Kynegion House....

In a world without heroes one man stands to real-fight in the fake-fight world of professional wrestling: Hero Gregoropolous. Only in this fake fight, he's fighting for his life. Really. For real. But in a fake-fight setting. Get it?

THE SQUARED CIRCLE

Where sports entertainment meets reality television—if

that reality television starred people like Rupert Pupkin and Alexandra Forrest. If I have to explain who they are, I hate you.

THE SQUARED CIRCLE

Some dreams were never meant to be lived. The ones that are nightmares. Like this one. Vague enough? Do I have to telegraph everything? Why aren't you intrigued yet? What's wrong with you?

THE SQUARED CIRCLE

This book has not yet been rated.

Free Space   Jeremy Vaeni

PLEASE ENJOY OUR FEATURE PRESENTATION

Free Space   Jeremy Vaeni

CHAPTER 1

August, 1999. The dog days. And the dogs are out, soaring down Fulton Avenue headed toward the Bingo Palace in sunny Sacramento. Prince's original hit single "1999" is blaring from the radio. Not the inferior remix version—the original 1982 jam.

These old dogs know how to party. Because they're not dogs, they're people. Stop being so literal-minded, that gets you nowhere in film. *My* film. A film so rich with subtext even Stanley Kubrick would... something. About Donald Trump. I'm not good with jokes, sorry.

Where do these Anubis-like people bus in from you ask? It's not an old age home, I can tell you that, because some of them aren't that old. But I won't tell you where they're from. Mystery is fun! Like Area 51 in Nevada. And Luis Garavito in Columbia. (That'll be funny when you look it up. Or at least inventive.)

"B-I-N-G-O! B-I-N-G-O! B-I-N-G-O! And Bingo was

their Gaaaame, oooooh!"

"Good times!"

"Hallelujah!"

Listen to them singing in rounds. Adding lyrics. Not even paying attention to Prince. Or me. Or the camera—or "Boom Mic" Mike, for that matter.

Good. This is good. This will look natural. It *is* natural. It's a documentary, duh. On bingo and the people who love to play. Thanks for playing along, Bingoers!

***

Okay, here we are pulling up to the Bingo Palace. It's early yet, only 6:00pm. Bingoers are doing the meet and greet thing. There's already long lines of people waiting for bingo cards, special bingo cards—yes, even more special game cards—and the early bird special. Some have already bought their cards and claimed their favorite spot along one of the long tables in a sea of them. Those people are ordering coffee and foodstuffs.

You can tell the real pros from the novices by their bingo paraphernalia: plastic cardholders, ink stamps from home, coffee thermoses filled with the good stuff. There is one early bird with stringy brown hair drizzling down her tie dye t-shirt who compulsively calls out, "Pull tabs! Pull tabs!"

Something about the way she puffs out her P sounds through her acne-scarred cheeks and the way the usher hurries to her with the pull tab cards reminds one of a momma jay spitting worm down the gullet of her screeching baby. Less messy than that, though. But just as natural.

"Can everybody hear me?"

That's the MC. He prefers not to tap on the mic and pop everyone in the ear with that annoying *Is this thing on?* sound. His years as the voice of the Bingo Palace have served him well. By that I mean he's a pro. By that I mean he knows what he's doing—not that women are tossing him their panties or anything. He's good; he's not Tom Jones good.

Still, about a third of the room responds with a drone of *Yes* so resounding you'd think the zombie apocalypse hit. (That was me being ironic, by the way.)

The MC tells them, "Good. We're going to start the early bird special for this evening. It's a two bingo any way and the first number is in the window."

On a large monitor, a ball reads, "I16." The early birds work diligently, blotting out all the I16s on their cards with their ink stamps. They look like my old man on tax day, some of them, the way they're frantically rifling through smears of papers spread out before them. Don't want to miss an I16.

Meanwhile, the stragglers in the back of the card

lines are getting antsy. They know they're missing out on potential big money with every round that goes by.

The whole scene reminds one (this one) that 1999 was a simpler time in America. Bush hadn't stolen an election yet, just on the cusp of that. We didn't have to pretend to know what a Muslim was. Cell phones weren't smart. Newspapers weren't computer screens. Books weren't computer screens. Computers weren't computer screens. And the weather didn't try to kill us every few weeks.

People were more innocent, more sheltered from the world, and slightly less aloof. But that doesn't mean it didn't suck. Oh, it sucked all right. Like a hooker vacuuming hooker juice. We'll get to that. (Not literally.)

Now come see my bedroom.

CHAPTER 2

Hello. Me again. Norm Plumber. Since I'm the man behind this little slice-of-life vignette, I thought I'd tell you a bit about myself. I am a twenty-five-year-old student of Jungian Psychology and an amateur filmmaker and a student of life. In this film I'm going to be documenting the town next to the one where I grew up. Everyone documents their hometown, but nobody ever documents the next town over. Plus, my parents don't like me. Or at least they don't want to be on camera. So my hometown's out, 'cause what's the point?

I wasn't going to include myself in the film at all, but I think it is important to realize that no documentary has a truly omniscient narrator. Unless I just left the camera rolling, and nobody wants that. For more on this issue please see Warhol, Andy.

So you see it is important to know whose POV—or point of view—you are watching. Mine. Norm's. Mine.

Warning: much to the chagrin of my grade school

21

classmates, I have forgotten about my lateral lisp. They used to call me Daffy Duck, but I sound more like Stan's sister Shelly in *South Park*, as evidenced by the fact that my friends now call me Shelly. Not all the time, just when they think I'm not listening.

Which is fine. I get it. The point is, I forget I sound like this because I'm me, but you might find it annoying after a while and leave me. Or stop watching, I mean.

Anyway.... Welcome to my bedroom!

I use a cameraman most of the time but since this is our intimate beginning together I thought I'd swing the cam around the room myself and show you some stuff that makes me the man I am today. Grand tour, people! Buckle up!

It's a bit cluttered but I didn't want to spoil the reality of everything by cleaning up. It's a mess; I'm a mess. Don't read too much into that.

Are those Michael Jackson posters fixed like a halo around his college diploma, you ask?—Yes. Don't read too much into that, either. I'm a big Michael Jackson fan. Still. He was innocent. All those people who said he molested that boy did it for money. From tabloids. Like CNN. But we never hear about that do we, Spanky?

That life-size monkey puppet hanging precariously by his plastic thumbs from my bookshelf is Spanky The

Monkey, Guardian of Tissues. See the box of Kleenex above his head? Yeah. He's my confidante for when I can't trust friends.

And—Oh!—and also, on the wall here, I forgot, is my Bachelor's Degree in Fashion Design. In case you were wondering. I'm done with school (hated school) and now I'm a filmmaker. But I like to remember my roots so I keep the degree on the wall. Plus, where else am I gonna put it, the trash?

Oo-oo! But Norm! I thought you said you were a student of Jungian Psychology?

Very good, Spanky. I wasn't clear on that issue. What I meant was that I've read a few books and find Carl Jung's— *Carl's*—approach to the human mind... novel. And now I realize I have some shadow work to do up here, where I'm tapping my temple.

Oo-oo! Oh.

Yeah. Maybe that is for what this film is for: documenting small town life kind of like what I grew up with, but one town over, to discover myself.

Why aren't I like them? I grew up next to them. Is it the fashion degree? Is it 'cause I hate bingo in a bingo town? My hometown is a bingo town too, but we don't brag about it. The game's secreted away in the basements of churches like clues to the Jesus bloodline. Possibly with them. There's no palace dedicated to it, in other words.

I'm just asking, no judgements, why would a whole town play bingo for fun out in the open like it's bowling or mini golf?

It's silly. It's all chance. Where's the challenge in chance? We don't believe in chance do we, Spanky?

Oo-oo! Speak for yourself!

Despite my concerns, mine is not to judge. Mine is to understand. Come with me now on a journey of understanding like no other. A journey that if this were a book and not a movie would have started here. Right here. Because I read somewhere that you're supposed to throw out, like, the first twenty pages of what you think is good writing because it actually sucks. Start with a point of crisis or something like that. But this is a documentary on bingo. It's all crisis if you know how to look.

CHAPTER 3

Gross. The MC called B3 and some White dude yelled bingo like there's a party in his pants and we're all invited. But that's not what's gross. I just saw an elderly woman in a wheelchair hooked up to a clear—that's right, a *clear*—colostomy bag three-quarters full. She was being raised up on a platform by what I understand is her personal nurse. But that's not what's gross. What's gross is, enough bingoers applauded her arrival that it drew my attention and I absentmindedly took a Funyun to the schnoz. Now I'm gonna be smelling that armpit smell the rest of the night. You can't get Funyun dirt out of your nose hairs, that's physically impossible. Gross.

"Hold on, folks, we have a possible bingo."

This place is packed with hopeful winners. They have to wait for an official to check that White guy's card to confirm the victory. The hall is so big and full of conversations that the MC needed to announce it through the sound system.

Listen to the moans! The sad, sad moans at someone else's victory! Tape's rolling. We're capturing all of this.

The official calls out, "Number two four three seven," and the MC, who speaks her language, responds, "Two four three seven. That's a perfect small stamp. That's a bingo."

The winner is practically high-fiving himself. He just won $250 cash. The MC asks if there are any other winners but the crowd is crickets. He says, "Hearing no other bingos, I declare this round over, leaving one lucky winner," and all watch enviously as the official lays down the big bucks.

The lady to the winner's right leans in and says to him, "You know you have to share that with the rest of the table, right?"

Those in the immediate vicinity chuckle. I take that as my cue to cut my first interview. I ask the winner, "How does it feel to win?"

He ponders a moment then says, "Like breeze in a fart hole: it just feels right." He breaks into an awkward laugh and I can tell by his teeth this money isn't going to a dentist.

I say to him, "Ah. A Hawthorne fan." I don't think he gets it. I don't think I get it either.

Rescued by a Latina mammi! She's a hot little number with a caboose enough for two folding chairs. She must be uncomfortable sitting in just the one with those toddlers toddling on her lap. She sees us and motions for the camera. We head over to see what her deal is, passing a junk food cart.

Know what would wash Funyuns down? Twinkies. I hear them calling to me with their sweet siren song, but I'm not falling for it. I swear I also hear that one early bird from before calling for pull tabs. "Pull tabs! ... Pull tabs!" She's like Rain Man begging for Wapner.

The elderly woman on the wheelchair throne's colostomy bag bubbles. The MC calls, "O sixty-eight." The Latina chick stares into the camera breaking the fourth wall as she asks me for what this is for.

"What's that?" I ask. I find the myriad diversions discombobulating.

"What's this for?" she repeats.

I tell her I'm filming a documentary on the bingo scene.

She says, "The bingo scene? Foolio, there ain't no bingo scene! Just poverty people trying to make ends."

"Why are you here?" I ask.

"I'm poverty people!" She barks this angrily then gives it a beat and breaks into a laugh. "No suh! I'm just fucking wit chu!" she admits.

I ignore the humor fail and ask, "Are these your children?"

"Yes. This is Natacha and the little one is Lizzy."

"They're beautiful," I tell her.

And they are.

"No doubt," she says.

This is going well.

"You must be a great mom to raise two children this well-behaved."

"I do my best but right now they're just tired from crying."

"Babies cry."

"Babies do cry. They do. Tonight, especially. I wouldn't have come here except my husband hit me."

Now she has what you might call a faraway look in her eye and I'm legitimately concerned. I ask her, "He did?"

"First and last time that man ever lays a finger on me," she says.

"Do you.... Should I turn off the camera and we can talk about it?"

"You a shrink?"

"I'm a student of Jungian Psychology. I'm here doing some shadow work."

"Does it pay?"

"It's some tough stuff but in the end it pays, yes."

She looks at me with... I dunno. An annoyed arrogance, if that makes sense. She hisses, "No, I mean does it *pay*."

"Not... not that. No, not money," I stutter.

She glares at me and says, "Nigga, why am I wasting my time wit chu? Get the two-step! A cute White couple just walked in; go interrogate them."

"Thank you for your time," I say. "If you need to talk...." I fish around my wallet for my card and hand it to her. She flicks it down on the table.

"Whateva."

That's what I think, too. Only when I think it I replace the second *a* with an *e* and an *r* and pronounce it correctly. I don't mean that judgmentally, that's just how I speak. Correctly.

We're going with the flow here and taking her advice, hurrying over to the new White couple, as she called them. I can't be certain but in the rush I could swear I just saw the elderly woman's colostomy sack bubble again. Why do I feel like every time I see that I die just a little bit inside, not her? (Well, her too. Old!)

"O seventy," the MC intones.

A woman offscreen yells "Bingo!" to the moaning chagrin of her fellows. I keep the camera trained on the young couple we're approaching just long enough to blurt, "Excuse me! Hey!" and then run out of tape.

CHAPTER 4

The camera man gets his tape situation figured out and the couple agree to let me interview them at their table. They are obviously outsiders, big city folk. It'll be good to get their impression of the small town bingo scene.

They're in from New York, which is cool. I'm gonna go there someday—probably to film festivals with this thing.

His name's Mark. He's got one of those fake tough guy accents, you know, like from *da Bronx*?

Her name's Sabina. I can't tell where she's from originally. But we're all from our moms, right? So in a sense, a very real sense, we're all from a damp and wonderful place called Vagina. I don't know if that's what the Buddhists mean by *oneness*, but they should look into it. Maybe even literally.

And our conversation goes something like this....

NORM

What is the craziest conversation you've ever overheard at a bingo parlor?

MARK

The craziest?—Let me think.

SABINA

Well we haven't—We don't play bingo.

MARK

—Often.

SABINA

We're from New York, so....

NORM

They don't have bingo in New York?

SABINA

Oh, yeah. They do somewhere I'm sure.

MARK

A lot of older people play.

SABINA

Yeah, I'm sure a lot of older people play bingo. Churches....

NORM

Mmm-hmm.

MARK

Craziest thing I ever heard?—You know what?

NORM

No.

MARK

Just the other day there was this fat chick, right? She turned
to the lady she was with and asked her which numbers were
odds and which ones were evens, 'cause the game was that
everyone gets to mark their odd numbers before playing.
Now look, bingo caters to the lowest denominator—I mean
you don't have to know shit to play bingo, that's the way it's
set up.

NORM

Right.

MARK

So to not know what the fuck odds and evens are is knowing
less than shit!

32

NORM

I hear what you're saying.

MARK

Everybody knows what odd numbers are: one, three, seven,

nine—

NORM

Five.

MARK

Right, five! I mean come on! You learn that before one plus

one is fucking two!

SABINA

Mark!

NORM

And this offends you.

SABINA

Honey, that's not fair! The poor girl was retarded!

MARK

No she wasn't!

SABINA

Yes she was! I sat next to her! That lady she was with was her mother! She has Down Syndrome!

MARK

Oh. Is that why she looked like that?

SABINA

Yes!

MARK

Huh.

(*short pause*)

Still though!

* * *

John, the owner of the Bingo Palace, offered me a handicapped bathroom stall to conduct interviews in. By the way peeps around us are staring, I think maybe I'll take him up on that. Safety first. Like condoms. Unless there's a pill. I am told.

CHAPTER 5

I can tell by the crackling static and feedback that something amazing is about to waft through the air like winds of change. "Stanley, your order is up. Stanley," a gravelly female voice on the PA system drones.

Stanley is the young White dude who won earlier. He moseys on over to the concession stand with a bounce in his step, ready for an extra dose of jalapeño poppers, but a young Black guy about his age stops him with a gentle yet firm hand on the shoulder. Stanley turns and the Black guy asks, "Hey, you the guy who got bingo?"

"Yeah, man," Stanley says. I wonder if he always says "man" or if it's an affectation for the African American's benefit.

"I'll see you in the parking lot." The Black guy does deadpan better than the PA system lady. Stanley looks like he's turning whiter. The Black guy laughs and lets him off the hook. "I'm just kidding! Good job, man, really." He extends his hand. Laughing along, Stanley shakes it.

"Thanks, man," Stanley says, barely concealing his relief.

I can barely conceal my glee. We are catching this. All of this. All of this brilliant drama and racial tension unfolding in realtime for viewers in the theater and at home and at the Golden Globes and at the Oscars, provided there are not a lot of Holocaust docs coming out next year.

The young Black man strides away. Stanley sees us. How could he not? We're right in his face. He turns to his left and confides in the camera. "That's not right. I'm no racist, but for a Black guy to even joke like that, it's just.... Especially after O.J.. That verdict still don't sit right with me."

This gets me to thinking about racism. There's a lot of different colors and shapes and breaths in this room. Shouldn't this, of all places, be a melting pot?

There's a smorgasbord of what sound like accents, yet the crowd is predominantly White and from America. It's the illusion of multiculturalism. Or maybe just undereducated.

Then again, who wants to sit in a room full of grad snoots playing bingo ironically? Not this fly on the wall, so I'm not complaining. But I am still confused.

Who better to help me sort this out than Marge, the rotund tan-skinned woman in the pink T-shirt rippling tightly over her well-earned folds? She is, after all, sitting to the right of Stanley, thus far our most controversial figure. I'll bet I can get her to speak candidly while Stanley regains his composure by the food counter. Now he knows why Donald Trump doesn't carry a wallet. Probably. Probably he has a Black guy carry it for him.

"Is there a lot of racism at bingo?" I ask Marge.

"No. No racism. We all get along pretty well here. *Yat*, we do... we do.... But that smoking section wins an awful lot, I'll tell ya what," she says. What is that accent? She pronounces *what* like *watt*. It's like Vermont meets *Dueling Banjos*. I can't quite place it and don't quite want to.

Did she just imply something about the smoking section?

"The... the smoking section?" I ask as confused as you might assume.

"Yat. Smoking section. The smokers," she says.

"You think the game is somehow rigged in their favor?"

"Oh, I dunno. Been playing here for twenty-three years and ever since they implemented that mandatory smoking section, I'll tell ya what."

She let's it hang. I can't. "What?"

She rolls her eyes. "They get more bingos over there!"

She might as well have called me stupid. Nobody likes stupid. That's why Adam Sandler's days are numbered.

Speaking of win, I need to win her trust back. "I feel what you are saying, I really do. You think the parlor is run by smokers," I state.

Her body language tightens up. Tightening is just what her body needs and so I'm glad to have provided that for her. "The world is run by smokers, son! The whole world ever since LBJ!" Then she relaxes. I think she knows I'm not the enemy here.

A grin creeps up her face and she says, "But other than that... it's a melting pot!"

"You need heat to melt things in a pot so... thank God for the smokers, right?"

She stares blankly into the lens.

"Maybe?" I ask.

Nobody home.

CHAPTER 6

Me and my crew finally had a spare moment to gussy up the handicapped stall in the men's room. I tried to erase some of the lewd graffiti but it just made a bunch of marker smears. It looks like *shart* deco in here. Windex helped with the smell and the seat cover is nice and dry now. The acoustics are phenomenal.

I never got that about bathrooms. Why would anyone want pitch-perfect reverb in the most disgusting room in the house? The bathroom is like the building's id and its walls sing the song of the shadow of the human organism. Why do we give the body's id voice and clarity yet suppress our psychological id? Perhaps these vignette interviews will reverse this. Or at least nobody better fart in here, cuz… gross.

***

Stanley has digested his poppers and is ready to go. Hopefully not *go*, go. Or if he does, warn us first?

STANLEY

What I love most about bingo is… the sense of community. Because where I grew up in South Carolina I actually watched my granddaddy give sheep the vote. So being around *womens* is healthy.

NORM

I feel… I feel what you're saying…. What are you saying?

STANLEY

It was like Viagra before Viagra for the old man, that farm.

NORM

So your life experience—which is valid and true for you—is that of witnessing your grandfather—

STANLEY

Lamb boning.

NORM

Lamb… right. And how did that make you feel?

STANLEY

Well I didn't count sheep at night, I can tell you that.

NORM

Mmm-hmm....

STANLEY

And I hate petting zoos.

I love this man. He has everything a Freudian could want. Shame I'm more of a Jungian guy. Still, I love this man!

CHAPTER 7

Okay, time to confront this Smokers Conspiracy head on.

We walk through the door of the glass wall that partitions the smokers' layer from the land of oxygen. From the nonsmoking side it looked like a leper colony being gassed. In the thick of the fog, though, you don't notice how much death your lungs are producing. In fact, from in here the nonsmoking section looks cloudy.

We approach Bobby-Jo, a boney middle-aged White woman with dirty blond hair drizzling down past her butt. She's yelling—practically dancing—"BINGO!"

She excitedly tugs on one of the tightly folded arms of her husband who does not stir underneath his ten gallon hat. I didn't even know they allowed those outside of Reno. I could have sworn that was Nevada state law. Or Texas. Or somewhere. Somewhere not in front of me.

"I see you've won bingo there." I don't like to brag but I kind of fancy myself a new age Studs Terkel—only I'm more everyman than he is. I just ask the obvious questions and let the interviewee take it from there. I find that people tend to open up easier when you don't come at them with an undercurrent of subtext. Then they create the subtext by virtue of not self-editing. Then I edit it because I'm also quite the editor. No biggie. Just another rare skill to keep humble about.

Bobby-Jo smiles big for the camera. "I'm so proud I could pop! Russell, we won! We won, honey!"

Russell sighs heavily and turns the other cheek, completely disinterested and almost frustrated, it seems like. His eyebrows look like furry caterpillars doing the wave in the shade and seclusion of that massive hat brim. His malaise doesn't stop her from hugging his arm.

"I was just telling Claire how I've been bingo-ing every night this week out on the Reservation, didn't win a dime, but look at me now! A winner!"

Claire looks like a chunkier version of Bobby-Jo. Her hair's a little shorter and her grin... mmm... not quite as toothy. Where Bobby-Jo has a pronounced overbite, Claire has jack o'lantern holes. She says to her friend, "Now you can afford that *pertty* new dress you been eyeing."

"Oh, I know! I'm gonna look like a million bucks for Russ Junior's graduation!"

I ask, "How much is the dress?"

"Eighty-five bucks," Bobby-Jo says, alternating her unsure gaze between me and the camera.

"How much did you win?" I ask.

"Two hundred and fifty bucks!"

"And do you play all the games?" I ask.

Claire interjects, "All the games all night!" And the two women whiff a sloppy high-five.

Bobby-Jo assures her she's next. "If I can win, you can too!" They high-five it again. Barely.

Their excitement is infectious. Still, I am immune.

"Just for clarity's sake, though, if you play every game, that runs you what? Twenty-nine dollars?" I ask this more to myself than either of them. I'm trying to do math in my head, not my strongest suit.

Bobby-Jo says, "Around there."

"So if you played and lost six days this week, that's a one hundred seventy-four dollar loss," I say.

"Yes but I won two hundred and fifty bucks!"

"No, you won seventy-six dollars. You're nine dollars short for that dress."

"No!" Bobby-Jo's not quite yelling but she is agitated.

Claire hates me, I think. She blurts, "No! She won two hundred and fifty dollars—Are ya thick?" like she's defending her friend's honor or something.

"Sorry. My deepest apologies, ladies. Sometimes my

shadow gets the best of me," I tell them. And I mean it. Claire gives Bobby-Jo a sideways glance. "His what?" she asks like a defendant consulting her attorney.

"My shadow. I'm doing shadow work," I offer cheerfully. They look perplexed.

Bobby-Jo says "Okay....?" Like a drawn-out question.

"It's tough stuff but it's definitely worth it. What do you think about the smokers winning more frequently than non-smokers?" I don't mean to change the subject rudely, but I figure if I can catch her off guard maybe she'll accidentally confess something. But she doesn't.

"Is that true?" she asks.

"It is true and therefore valid to the non-smokers," I explain.

"Well, I ain't heard nothing about that."

The cameraman pans to Claire who simply says, "No."

"Do you think it's a conspiracy?" I ask.

"Now I just told you I ain't heard nothing about it! How can I have an opinion about something I don't know?"

Claire ribs her and says, "You just won. Maybe there is a conspiracy." Then she blows smoke into the camera and both women crack up like the first time they ever heard about the chicken getting to the other side.

Bobby-Jo chases their cackling with, "Well if there is

I ain't in on it."

I know she's telling the truth and I want her to know that I know, so I say, "That's for sure! Or else you wouldn't have lost a hundred seventy-four dollars in six days!"

"That was on the Indian Reservation, not here!" Bobby-Jo corrects.

"So for clarity's sake, you—a smoker by choice—lose one hundred seventy-four dollars at another bingo hall over a six-day period, then come here and win right out of the gate. I ask you again, is this not a conspiracy?"

Claire and Bobby-Jo scramble to holler *No!* over each other, then Bobby-Jo tells me, "No it ain't! It ain't at all. You're a fine confection, Sugar."

"I'm just trying to figure some things out. Like Kenny Rogers. He was the Rambling Man."

"Well, take your negative energy outside; this is the winner's table tonight!"

"Not if you buy that dress. Then you're down nine dollars."

"Get out!" they yell in unison.

Claire's got crazy eyes. I'd love to know her story. I think this and faintly hear the call of the pull tabs woman in the nonsmoking section.

"Pull tabs! Pull tabs!" She's like a parrot, that sweet old bird.

I'm about to press my luck and ask Claire for a private interview in the bathroom stall confessional... and that's when I see her. Out of the corner of my periphery—my periphery's periphery—through the haze, I see her glide into the smoking section. Bingo cards stick out of her large orange pocketbook; a Virginia Slim dangles off her bottom lip; she shakes her ink blotter like it's the shaft of a man. Of all men. Of me....

She passes me a sly glance like she knows something about me and is intoxicated with what she knows. Like we're in on a secret together and that secret is our future but also our deep past. Did we know each other in a previous life?

Her fading strawberry blonde perm all tied up in a bun; her fuck-me red lipstick symmetrically lined on her forever pouty lips; her Impostor Perfume wafting from the silk of her skin—especially, I imagine, around the costly breast region, of which she is ample, and the frontal nether region, which is more than likely shaven in the form of a lowercase "l." This morsel of walking, breathing sultriness breaks the monotony of stale cigarettes and spent pipe.

Oh, she is perfect. She's too perfect. And for a moment the camera crew and I are stunned as she swishes her hips like a model all the way to her seat. They see what I'm seeing. There's no need to verbalize it.

I snap out of it and tap "Boom Mic" Mike on the arm

while jerking my head at the camera man. Together, we navigate through the sweaty mob toward this seductive goddess, a beacon in the cancerous fog.

As I stare for too long, I can't help but wonder how many grades she spent cheerleading in high school and if she made it to college. No, actually I didn't wonder that last part.

"Dude, watch the mic! Get the boom mic out of the —" Even as I bitch about the microphone dangling in the shot, "Boom Mic" Mike is on it, withdrawing his thick black tube from the frame. "—shot. Thanks. Lets keep it professional, guys."

The cameraman positions himself perfectly to capture her at the least-jaundiced angle beneath the fluorescent ceiling lights. She greets us with a warm, expectant smile but suddenly the camera veers in the hands of a young boy who wants to make goofy faces into the lens.

"Hey there, fella!" I say, a bit surprised, but also loud enough so that his mother, who isn't paying attention, sees all this. She does and she slaps his hand. I kinda wish that part didn't happen.

The child relinquishes control back to the camera man but looks like he's at that in-between state, unsure whether or not to cry. Will it get him attention? Will it get him in further trouble? He alternates his glassy eyes between his mother and us.

"Jimmy, stop that!" his mother scolds.

Then Jimmy's slightly older sister taunts him. "Yeah, Jimmy, stop that!"

"That's fine, ma'am," I assure the woman. She's busy playing bingo. She doesn't need the hassle of loving her children.

"He needs to relearn what's good touch and what's bad touch is," she tells me.

"Re—ah—re—Did you say *relearn*?"

"They lived with their uncle for a while." I wait for further elucidation but apparently that says it.

"Playing bingo?" I ask. Again with the obvious. Interviewing, like nation-building, is about winning hearts and minds.

"Won twice this week!" She's proud, clearly.

"Twice, huh? And you're a smoker. Coincidence?" I'm only half joking. "Boom Mic" Mike chuckles offscreen causing the mic to bob in and out of the shot. I scold him to watch it.

"Am I missing something?" The mother asks this, and later, when I look at the footage, I see that the cameraman chose to slow zoom on her gummy meth mouth. At least someone's doing his job right.

At the present moment, though, all I see is mouth. I

can't signal to zoom in on it so I just kinda pray about it for a second and hope that we create our own reality. Mine. And we do. Like I just told you. But I didn't find out until later. I told you that, too.

Off camera a woman says, "Let me guess...."

Me and my crew whip around to face the voice. *Her* voice. *Her* face. I am face to face with *her* face. Delicious.

She waits for the cameraman to steady his grip before finishing her thought. Then, "You're Oliver Stone here to solve the great Smokers Conspiracy?"

"Nope. If I were Ollie Stone I'd be filming this at the Reservation with fourteen different film stocks and you'd be played by a dark and tawdry Christina Ricci," I quip. We both giggle like school girls. This is going well.

"You're crazy!" she tells me.

"No. I just have some issues. But then this isn't about me, it's about you."

"Me?"

"All of you, yes."

"Rumor has it you're here doing shadow work. Is that true?"

"Who told you that?"

"Marge over in non-smoking. You're all anyone's talking about over there. They want to know what the hell *shadow work* means."

"What does it mean to them?"

"Nothing real. Big city talk. They think you're here to poke fun at us."

"Why would I do that?"

"Money. Fame. Whatever this is for."

"Oh I don't need to make fun of you for that." I reveal this and hear distantly like an echo of an echo, "Pull tabs! ... Pull tabs!"

"That's what I told her. I assumed by *shadow work* you meant the repressed traits you've buried in your unconscious mind," my mystery woman says.

"You're familiar with—?"

"Surprise! I went to therapy too you know."

"Would you like to talk about it?" I ask. Poop, I thought maybe she was hitting on me.

"Not here. After bingo if you still care." Yes! She *is* maybe hitting on me!

"I care. And I... I feel what you're saying."

"Do you?"

"Don't I?"

"Do you?"

"Don't I? Listen, can I—can *we* follow you around for a day, like a day in the life of...?" I ask.

She twirls her red ink blotter between her fingers like a hard rock drummer. "That may be the only way you can make this little project, or whatever, not be about you," she says.

"What does that mean?" I ask.

"It means yes."

CHAPTER 8

A new day is upon us, as those who speak in the passive voice like to say. We are no longer at the Bingo Palace but in the palace of my new and favorite princess, Mandy-Alise. She is a former stripper who has done quite well for herself. She owns her own house in the sticks off the highway.

It's morning when we arrive and I persuade her to climb back into bed so we can film her starting her day. I want to see her wake, yawn, stretch—fart if she has to. I want reality.

There are annoying traffic sounds in the distance. I'll probably overdub some chirping bird effects to make it sound more natural.

Later, we record her for a voiceover. Just a little bit of scripting I whipped up for her to capture who I imagine she is on the inside, beneath the bad decisions and the need for attention.

She reads my words: "Each morning I wake up fresh,

new, and alive, like a moth from its cocoon. Or a very smart Buddha."

"—Good!" I'm pleased with her performance. It's my fault we have to do several takes. I can't help but whisper her lines underneath her.

I also stage her swinging open the double doors of her bedroom so we can take in the splendor that is her classically white trash living space. (I mean that in a good way!) It is filled with trinkets that are meaningful to her mixed indiscriminately with trinkets that cost less than five bucks. Here is where I'll place the other bit of voiceover script, where she says, "Each day brings me that much warmth. That much joy. That much closer to realizing my dream of becoming Mandy-Alise, Bingo Queen."

And then, *BOOM!* the chirping birds CD will skip and we'll roll the title:

"FREE SPACE: THE REAL LIFE STORY OF A BINGO QUEEN"

Beneath that...

FADE IN:

"A NORM PLUMBER EXPERIENCE"

I can totally envision how all of this will play. After the title, we'll cut to Mandy taking us through the kitchen, allowing us to explore her rooms in the intimate way one (this one) imagines her former regulars at the strip club still wish they could.

"This is my kitchen. I'm an average woman of average means. See? Dishes in the sink. I'm gonna eat waffles and watch *Springer*." She actually says this. One is not imagining it. (This one.)

"Then what?" I ask.

"Then bathe and off to work."

"Oh, God bless you, Baby Jesus."

Is she really going to let us film her bathing ritual? Is this going to be the greatest film alive?

Not... not that film is alive. Necessarily. Not with our current technology, anyway. Who knows what the future will bring, though?

Why am I thinking about that?—My future is now!

CUT TO:

BINGO PALACE - MEN'S BATHROOM CONFESSIONAL. RECORDED YESTERDAY.

MARGE

I ain't never been in no men's room before. A lady could really get used to this.

NORM

We cleaned it up a bit. It's not usually this *Windexy*.

MARGE

I gotcha.

NORM

So tell us—and don't look at the camera; either look at me or look right here above the camera, if you would—tell us what brings you back to the Bingo Palace over and over and *over* and over again.

MARGE

Bingo is inspiring. It's like reading Oprah's book of the month. And when you win... oo-oo! Gives me the gurgling shits just thinking about it!

NORM

Would you say there's no other feeling like it?

MARGE

Yes. Definitely.

(*thinks about it*)

Well, there was at one time but that was two husbands ago.

(*a long beat*)

And here I'm talking about my twat.

NORM

Gotcha.

CHAPTER 9

Ho. ly. Poop sticks. Mandy is standing before me wearing a pink terrycloth bathrobe, and from what I can see, not a thing else. She drew herself a bubble bath while I wrestled the camera from my cinematographer. If we're going to do this right it has to be intimate. There has to be trust on her part. I don't assume that just because she was a stripper she's comfortable shedding her clothes in every setting. It's just me and her, the way God intended it. Anything more by way of crew would be misogynistic and I don't want this scene to be about that.

"You sure you want to do this?" I ask her.

"No biggie," she says.

She drops the robe. Her pubic hair is shaven into a fine strip not at all unlike the letter "l."

"Oh my god! The lowercase l!" The words escape my better judgment and blow out my mouth, but she doesn't care. She smiles that tight-lipped *I know you want this* smile she must have learned while honing her dance craft.

She eases into the steaming bathtub like Prince in the *When Doves Cry* video. Every bit as sexy minus the hairy chest plus a couple inches in height. No doves. No prowling across the floor like a filthy panther. Yet.

"That feels so much better," she says. She groans when she stretches out in the massaging foamy water.

I'm praying my lens doesn't fog. It doesn't. There's one point for God. Make that two. D's, by the looks of them. And talk about buoyancy. Her breasts would make excellent arm floaties for children learning to swim.

Where were we?

"Describe what it is that makes you feel better," I maturely direct.

She looks at me like I'm a dope. "That would be the, ah, bubbles on my skin, Norm." She says this playfully, kind of snickers as she hands me a bar of creamy not-soap and turns over, hiney up. "Do my back."

"No! Can't. Camera." I drop the soap in its dish. I am a professional.

"What's the matter? You afraid?"

"Can't. Camera. What is it about you—That is to say, why—How are you so free with your body?" I ask.

"Um, I used to be a titty dancer, so...."

"I see."

"Yeah. Made a ton of mullah doing that."

"Why did you give it up?"

Mandy spins back around. Her quarter dollar nipples play peekaboo in the bobbing tidal foam. She plays hard to get with the camera, never quite looking into the lens or at me when she tells us, "Well, I—When I was a little girl growing up I was sexually abused by my father."

Which is not what I expect to hear.

"I'm sorry," I say.

"Molested. No, well, it wasn't you, thanks. But anyway, last year I realized I needed help because I would get these horrible panic attacks and I could never hold a steady relationship with a man and.... I was pretty much a wreck. So I started going to therapy and that helped a lot."

"It can be very therapeutic," I offer.

"It was.... It was.... And what it helped me realize is that all my problems are me. If you put me in a room with a thousand normal healthy guys and one abusive turd, I'll pick the shit-head every time."

"Mmm-hmm...." I wonder if I should drop the camera and pick up a notebook. Clearly sexy time has turned into therapy time. This I am used to.

She continues as if I'm not wondering anything. "Because I'm a man hater. Or should I say, *was* a man hater. I wanted them to want to fuck me. I needed them to treat me like shit because that reconfirmed in me the notion that all men are scum."

"Searching for Daddy," I say.

"Search and destroy; search and destroy. That was my game for the longest time, but you know what lay underneath it all? Self-loathing. I didn't hate men. I hated me."

"So for clarity's sake, beneath your attraction to men lies a hatred of men; beneath men lies you; and beneath you lies—?"

"My father."

"Your father. I feel what you are saying. And what about now?"

"Now I'm not so panicky but I still haven't met Mr. Right."

"Do you find yourself still trying to control men still?"

She looks at me, finally, kind of disdainfully, I think. Like almost with a wink she says, "You're here aren't you? Did you see my pussy by accident?"

"So you have a ways to go. Are you in therapy now?" I ask.

"No. After I gave up stripping I couldn't afford it."

CHAPTER 10

"Two cheeseburger combo meal and a large black cow. Will that be all?"

What is it I find so sexy about a defeated woman handing off bags of feed to animal families at the drive-thru window of a fast food dive? Is it her hair netted in a baseball cap? Is it her bought breasts caged in red and mustard uniform? Is it the sweat mingling with grease in the air settling on her skin?

No. I know what it is. It's her smile. A smile that began as defiance when she started the job, a temporary part-time gig while she was between goals, and ended as acceptance when it became a permanent forty-hour workweek. I think Mandy lived rough and never frowned. I think that's what I love.

"This is where I work. It's a big ol' grease pit," she admits with a laugh, "but people seem to want to eat it."

Mandy demonstrates some of her chores for the camera. I could watch french fries sizzling in a vat of hot lard all day long.

"This is the fryolator," she says. "Mmm! Yummy! Customers sometimes complain about the grease and I just tell them, 'Easy in, easy out!' Pollute your body at your own risk."

Although her boss agrees to let us film in his establishment, it isn't until her lunch break that she's allowed to have a real conversation.

"If I had kids I would never let them eat this shit," she confides, twirling a fry in her mouth for emphasis.

"But that one meal comes with a toy inside!" My glee is genuine.

She says, "If you have to bribe your kids to eat it, it can't be good for them."

"Even broccoli?" I wonder aloud.

Her manager holds up his left hand, fingers spread wide. Fat. Bald. A murky emotional presence. I can't believe he's got a wedding band on. Someone married him? Who married him? I smell a sequel.

"What's that?" I ask Mandy.

"That's Rex my boss telling me I got five minutes 'til my break's over," she explains.

"Do you get along?" I ask.

"With Rex? How many Rex's do you know?"

"None personally."

"How many do you think you would get along with? There are fifteen-year-olds working the registers who have more common sense than Rex."

"And he is the boss of you?"

"That's the tragedy of it all. The six-fifty an hour tragedy."

"Isn't that always the way?" I say.

I bite into my bun and pickles guest starring meat.

CUT TO:

BINGO PALACE - MEN'S BATHROOM CONFESSIONAL. RECORDED YESTERDAY.

RUSSELL
Hate bingo; can't stand it. Four hours and a half. Sitting on my duff. I don't get it. *Titanic* wasn't even four hours and a half long and it had a shipwreck and a gun chase.

NORM
And Leo.

RUSSELL
Who?

NORM

Leonardo DiCaprio.

RUSSELL

Was he the scrawny gay fella or the dude in the eyeliner?

JUMP CUT

RUSSELL

My wife drags me here, by gum! Says it's good for us to get out once in a while.

NORM

Leisure time can be extremely therapeutic.

RUSSELL

I suppose that's why I watch *Frasier*.

NORM

Have you heard of this alleged Smokers Conspiracy?

RUSSELL

Conspiracy?—Ha! That's a laugh. What about all the smokers who lose? What about me? I gotta sit there and I never win nothing. No, you wanna hear the only truth there is to know about bingo?

(*leans in, whispers*)

It's the whole reason them aliens use the anal probe.

NORM

Aliens?—Canadians?

RUSSELL

No! Them little gray fellas with the bald heads and the wraparound eyes, like on that show. What was that show?

NORM

The McLaughlin Group?

RUSSELL

Nope.

NORM

Oh, *Sightings.*

RUSSELL

(*nods*)
Great show. Informative.

NORM

I'll say.

RUSSELL

Yeah, so them aliens monitor us on their LCD screen displays up there in space and they see there are two types of people in this world: city folk and country folk. City folk cram themselves together; country folk needs space. Now let me inform ya, when you're stuck together with a whole bunch of strangers, what's the one thing you want to be?

NORM

Not claustrophobic.

(*laughs*)

RUSSELL

Smarter than everyone else.

NORM

Hmm?

RUSSELL

Smarter than everyone else. That's why country people is so dumb! We can afford to be! I ain't got nothing to prove out here in the free space! But unfortunately not everybody out here agrees with me.

NORM

They're in denial.

RUSSELL

About being dumb. So they gather together and play this....
What's the word?

NORM

Ludicrous.

RUSSELL

Ludicrous game that nobody in their right mind would
spend four hours and a half playing just so's they can yell,
"Bingo! Bingo!", win a stipend, and feel smart! Smart?! The
game ain't nothing but dumb luck!

NORM

What about the aliens?

RUSSELL

The aliens—the Grays—see this. They know what's going on
'cause they're.... Shoot, what's the word?

NORM

Third-person omniscient.

RUSSELL

No. I don't know. Anyway, they see what the deal is and they decide it's easier to abduct jerkwater country folk than intelligent city folk. Less witnesses, too.

NORM

Why are they abducting people in the first place?

RUSSELL

Genetic materials. They're creating a hybrid race.

NORM

Of us and them.

RUSSELL

Correct.

NORM

But they're taking the stupid jerkwater us's genetic stock. Wouldn't that dumb down the hybrids?

RUSSELL

That's why they use the anal probe! To wake us up! Bring us

up to speed.

NORM

That would do it!

(*laughs*)

Seriously.... *Does* probing someone anally make them
smarter or... or bring them out of denial?

RUSSELL

(*thoughtfully*)

No. I suppose it don't.... But if you could stick a prod up
some dumb guy's ass, would you do it?

Long pause.

NORM

Russell, you may be the wisest man who ever lived.

RUSSELL

(*smiles bashfully*)

Thank ya.

CHAPTER 11

I take in Mandy's living room while my crew films her unwinding with a smoke and a glass of Riunite on the love seat. It's early evening now and we've been with her all day. She's been a great sport about this. I wonder if she thinks she's getting paid. I mean, we had that talk privately. I told her there's no money in it for her. I can't help but think that in the back of her mind she's holding out hope for a surprise check.

Surprise! No check. I'm going to be up to my ears in credit card debt as it is. Plus, isn't it time strippers gave back? Their champaign room fees are outrageous.

"Normally what I do after work is take some *me* time to loosen up before bingo," she tells me.

I'm only half listening, far and away more interested in the meticulous clutter of her shelves: framed photos of her smiling with friends in various vacation scenes, little dolls, a glass swan.

I respond on autopilot. "Would it be fair to say that

bingo is your life?"

"Not until they applaud when I walk into the room like they do Ethel."

That grabs me. I turn to her, askance, like, *Do you mind if I share the love seat with you?* She rolls her eyes up to one corner, while jerking her mouth down the opposite corner, and reflexively shakes her head, *No fucking way.* I take that to mean she stinks of fries and horse meat and is embarrassed by the aftermath of her work shift. I pat the air in response letting her know I'm cool with giving her her space.

I understand Mandy. I sense that she understands I understand. Perhaps that's the real reason she agreed to do this.

"Ethel is the elderly lady with the colostomy bag," I confirm. Exposition has its place and this is it.

"Yes. I hope to dethrone her someday."

"You could push her off her wheelchair."

"That's foul!"

"I'm joking of course."

"I wouldn't joke like that if I were you, people might think things."

"What things?"

"Bad things."

"We cannot control what others think, Mandy, but

I'm not too worried about it in this case because they won't even hear my voice."

"What do you mean? You're editing yourself out?"

Why does she sound so shocked?

I plop down next to her because this conversation may take a while and I want her to know that I think she's beautiful no matter what she smells like. If I were directing an actress I'd have to literally tell her she's beautiful if she was feeling insecure in front of the camera. Over and over tell her this until she got over her camera shyness. But this is a documentary. All I can do is infer with my body language.

As I land, she feels the need to scoot over to her own cushion. To the far edge of it. Like nearly riding the armrest. I infer from her body language that she is a touch obsessive-compulsive and might have boundary issues. I mentally note all that and then unpack my explanation: "Of course. Except for the opener and some key narration sequences I have in mind I shouldn't be in this at all."

"Why? Why take yourself out?"

"This is a professional documentary. I want this to be big time. I can't explain everything as I go along and ask all the questions and stuff like that, 'cause the film should speak for itself. People being people, that's what this is. It isn't a play, it's a film. It's not a radio broadcast, it's a film. And as such, it should speak for itself."

She whips off her baseball cap and flicks it onto the coffee table with a look of annoyance, like she'd forgotten it was stuck to her skull all this time. "If you want my opinion, I think that's stupid, no offense," she says.

She waves her hair around and frizzes it out with her hands. I think she understands she looks gross and is on camera. She's annoyed, clearly, and taking it out on me, *clearlier*.

That which I understand cannot bother me and I let her know this level of me with my words: "None taken. If I were doing this for you, I would take that into consideration. No offense."

"None taken. I still think it's foolish, though. No offense," she says.

We both stare at each other for a solid few uncomfortable moments. It's a special place, mutual discomfort. When you're there you know that there is both linear time and only now happening at once.

I let us off the hook with, "So Ethel's the reigning Bingo Queen?"

"Hmm?—Yeah. The old dinosaur always wins. But more importantly she's been there forever. It's more of a respect thing."

"You want to be respected."

"I want to be noticed for something other than my

tits." She laughs at herself and that laugh hides a lot. I ignore it.

I say, "I noticed Ethel has a tracheotomy."

Mandy takes a drag of her cigarette. Says, "Too many years in the smoking section I guess." Then exhales.

I don't think that was deliberate.

"It's sad," she continues.

"Are you afraid that will be you someday?"

"Not at all."

"Why not?"

"Because I know my limits. I know when to say when, so to speak. Sometimes I think bingo is the only reason the broad is still kicking. But you know all dogs have their day. One day soon it'll be off with her head. In a good way."

"Starting at the hole in her throat," I offer.

"—Sick!"

"—I didn't mean it like that!"

"—And there will be a new queen."

"You."

"Me."

I nod to my camera guy. He pulls focus to a makeshift board game sitting on a table behind her, like we'd agreed.

"I was snooping around here earlier and I noticed

you have what looks like a homemade board game," I reveal.

Mandy grabs it and displays it for the camera. "This?" she says.

"Yes. What is that?"

She's suddenly alive with joy. "That's my board game!" Houston, I think we've stumbled across her passion.

"Your—"

"My board game that I made. I'm very excited about it, it's a combination of Truth Or Dare, Hangman, and the Magic 8-Ball."

"What's it called?"

"I call it Sexecutioner's Noose. It's an adult party game, ages seventeen and up."

"So you're a junior inventor," I announce.

"I'm a major inventor—ain't nothing junior about my shit! Years ago I came up with a telephone ringer that can sample sounds so instead of ringing, your phone could meow like a cat or scream, "Get the phone, bitch!"

"Could it yell bingo?" I ask in my studied Barbara Walters *Let's get back to business* tone.

"Whatever your beady heart desires," she says. And she pokes me in the heart with her finger. On the love seat. It's crazy how staged this feels.

"Actually, haven't I heard of that ringer thing before?" I ask.

"Yip, betcha have. The invention people I brought it to stole my idea 'cause I didn't have a working prototype. What am I a fucking engineer?—I was a titty dancer at the time!"

"So, *not* an engineer?"

"Far from it." She laughs as she thinks about it. "Not so far, but far."

CUT TO:

BINGO PALACE - MEN'S BATHROOM CONFESSIONAL. RECORDED YESTERDAY.

In the hot seat is JESSE, the Black man whom Stanley found threatening.

JESSE

Peoples of Earth! My name is Jesse and I love bingo! I love to win! I love to lose! I even love the smell of the place! ... Well, maybe not so much to lose.... Favorite food?—jalapeño poppers. Favorite game?—black out. No pun intended. You could say I am passionate about my bingo nights.

(*holds up ink blotter*)

See this? This is my dick. My dick is red because red's my favorite color. When I press my dick gently to the bingo cards, you know your ass is fucked!

(*laughs*)

I don't know what else to say, man—What do you want me to say?

NORM

My grandfather on my mother's side—my mother's father—was a nice man in all respects but one: he was extremely racist.

JESSE

Surprise, surprise, White boy!

NORM

Yeah. He used to say that Blacks would still be swinging from trees if it wasn't for us. And my grandmother, bless her heart, would say, "Well what about that Bill Cosby? You love that Bill Cosby!" It was awkward.

Short pause.

JESSE

Why did you just tell me that?

NORM

I'm doing what is called owning my own guilt, ah, in terms of race and my family and... and our heritage, really.

JESSE

Is that right?

NORM

No, it's wrong. It's all wrong. Small Pox to Indians and slavery to you people.

JESSE

Me people?

NORM

And genocide. God, who is the White man? .... Who does he think he is?

(*sighs in deep relief*)

Whoa boy! This has been a real cleansing experience for me! Thanks for letting me share it with you.

JESSE

(*in a serious tone*)

Yeah, this is special for me too. I never thought the opportunity would present itself for me to say this out loud, but.... You are one special cracker.

NORM

Really?

JESSE

Absolutely.

NORM

Is that good? Like slang? Like calling me yo nigga?

JESSE

Yo, shut the fuck up!

CHAPTER 12

I can tell by the way Mandy says, "I'm gonna take a quick shower and be right out," that it is a lie. The tell? She's female.

I'm trying to follow her in there but she's rudely jamming the door into my knee. "What are you doing?" she barks in annoyance.

"You're showering. It's for the movie." Because, *duh*. That's not me being mean, by the way, that just is what it is.

"Oh no, this shower's private," she says.

"But before when you were bathing—"

"You only need one nude scene for this thing to sell and that's as much as you're gonna get out of me. Go take a break, I'll be out in ten minutes."

She slams the door on me and the camera and blurts a promise we both know she won't keep. "Less! I'll be real quick!"

An hour later she walks out of the bathroom showered and blowdried, dressed and ready. Almost ready.

All but the perfume and makeup.

"There! See? Let me put on my face and we're good to go." This she says as if an hour didn't go by. Like it really was only ten minutes. That's girl time.

I've given the camera back to the camera man. I've directed him to shoot everything, even the stuff that really sounds like it should be off camera. Sometimes a documentarian's best work comes when no one's looking. That's how you end up with a *Faces of Death* series.

"Mandy, we need to talk." I've always wanted to use that line and here I got to mean it.

She's sitting at her beauty flip mirror that has a normal reflective side and a Bozo clown mirror on the other to pop zits and burn ants. She regards me, barely, with her eyes in the magnified Bozo side and says, "Do it while I'm putting on lipstick."

I decide we should shoot this right, so I wait for the camera man to position himself for the perfect confrontational shot: down below my chin when I speak, and then bird's eye-ish when the camera's on Mandy. It's a lot of squats but he can use the exercise.

"I love putting on the finishing touches before a game. It makes me feel whole. Completed, you know? Like I can take on the world!" she tells us.

"Great. Listen, I think we need to set some healthy

boundaries on our relationship."

"Okay...."

"Yeah, maybe I wasn't too clear about this but this is my film and so I would appreciate it if you would refrain from trying to direct it. No offense."

"You lost me—What?"

"I'm a professional. Okay, this is what I do. I don't need you telling me—"

"You told me you were an amateur filmmaker, you said that yourself."

"'Amateur' in the sense that I haven't made a lot of movies."

She stops with the eyeliner and swivels to face me. "What other sense is there, Norm? This is your first film!"

"Right," I confirm.

"Anyway, continue."

"My point is, I'll be the judge of how many nude scenes I need; how I conduct my interviews; how much—"

"Is this about not watching me shower?"

"No!"

"—Mr. Voyeur? You think just because I showed my who-who once, you're entitled?"

"I didn't say that!"

I can see the Egyptian head wiggles with the angry finger swirls coming a mile away.

"How much are you paying me for this?"

She does not disappoint.

"Nothing."

"That's right. Now you already got something for nothing so don't push your luck!"

"This isn't about me!"

She motions for me to talk to the hand. I hate that.

"Not another word," she says while averting my eyes.

"But—"

"Not a—!"

"You don't—"

"Not a la—!"

"You don't—"

"Naw-la-la—! Naw-la-la-la—! Take the camera and go work on your shadow or something."

Wow. That really did just happen. I can't exactly explain what just happened but it really did just.

"That's not a very healthy response," I say. Admittedly, I'm fishing.

"You want me to make the fucking 'I' statement, Norm? If-I-am-fucking-late-for-fucking-bingo-I-will- fucking-kill-fucking-you! Fucking-clear-fucking?"

She draws out her words like I'm a child. But not like I'm really a child—she knows I'm not. It's in the asshole way one does such things to make you feel like a child. Which I'm not. She knows that.

Unperturbed, I say, "Clear. But I'm not a perv. But you could wear a miniskirt."

She snaps her fingers toward the door. I turn to leave but then double check.

She fires, "Now!" at me.

"For the film!" I plead.

"Tootles, Jar-Jar!" She doesn't just say it, she mocks my lateral lisp as she says it and that fucking hurts... so good!

My artistic instincts tell me we're filming gold here!

CHAPTER 13

It's getting late in the evening and Mandy is driving us to bingo. I have a feeling she's fashionably late a lot, which is strange because this isn't exactly a fashionista event. My camera man has his Cannon DV cam trained on her from the passenger seat. I'm in the back nestling my face between them. I pray that the image stabilization feature on the camera will compensate for the failing shocks on her Corolla.

"How are you feeling?" I ask.

She's all business, eyes on the road. "Fine," she says.

"Okay?" I ask. I feel a tension but I cannot pinpoint why.

"I'm feeling fine, yes," she says.

"Excited?"

"Sure."

"You mad at me?"

"No."

"Would you tell me if you were?"

"Maybe."

"Would you?"

"Maybe."

The camera stays trained on her while I take a breather to formulate my next question. She's not playing music, which is nice because that might be a nightmare in licensing fees, depending on what's playing. I'm not really sure how that works but if a major studio like LionsGate or Troma picks this up, I won't have to worry about it.

Oh! I know what to ask!

"Would you?"

"Yes, all right?! I'd tell you!"

She's all manic with her hands. I really wish she'd stay ten and two but I don't want to tickle the panther so I keep it to myself. Instead I say, "Okay. A relationship's fertility thrives upon the nourishment that is open communication, Mandy. Remember that."

"Gotcha, Norm—Will you drop it?"

"Consider it dropped.... So how do you feel about tonight?"

"Fine."

"Yeah? You think you're gonna win?"

"Hope to."

"I'm rooting for you, Mandy.... Mandy?"

She sighs deeply like she knows my question before I

do.

"Are you mad at me?" I ask.

I can't believe this—she's ignoring me! "Are you? ... Are you? ... Huh?"

For the rest of the ride she grips the wheel ten and two. Firmly. I think she might still be mad at me still.

CUT TO:

BINGO PALACE - MEN'S BATHROOM CONFESSIONAL. RECORDED YESTERDAY.

An intimate chat with Mark sans his partner, Sabina.

MARK
I told you I don't play bingo.

NORM
Would it be fair to assume that you are in bingo denial?

MARK
Why, because I'm denying it?
(*scoffs*)

NORM

What is the first thing that pops into your head when I say
the words "Smokers Conspiracy?"

MARK

*The X-File*s? I don't know, man, come on.

NORM

Ever heard of it?

MARK

Nope.

NORM

Let's move on....

MARK

(*checks Swatch*)

Yeah, let's. Sabina's waiting for me. You said this would only
take a minute.

NORM

Sabina is your girlfriend?

MARK

Fiancée.

89

NORM

I see. Tell us what first attracted you to her.

MARK

It's stupid.

NORM

There are no judgments here, Mark, only people being
people. Who is to blame for that?

MARK

Well... back in New York she was working the counter at this
earthy crunchy granola shop. I had just come in from the
rain to buy some au naturel shit for my girlfriend at the
time—

NORM

So this was the first time you two had met?

MARK

Second. I'd gone in there twice when she was there. But this
time she was wearing a half shirt and when she bent down to
grab something under the counter—I think it was a bag or
something.... Yeah, a bag—I noticed she had a little butterfly

tattoo on the small of her back.

Short pause.

NORM
Mmm-hmm.

MARK
(*bursts*)
That's fucking sexy!

NORM
Oh, I agree. A tableau on the small of the back depicting the most beautiful of all insects exiting the underworld where lives the Sacred Feminine, who has graced the bug with sweet freedom through metamorphosis, and renewed its purpose, is oft-times the most overlooked and yet most erotic feature of tattooed Woman.

MARK
No shit, dude! It's right by the crack!

NORM
Yeah.

MARK

Of the ass!

NORM

Yes.

MARK

The ass is fucking awesome in general, but her ass is the
shit! I knew right there, right precisely at that moment, it
was love.

NORM

What about the other girl you were seeing?

Mark holds up four fingers.

NORM (CONT'D)

What's that?

MARK

Four.

NORM

Four?

MARK

Four.

Norm waits for him to say four of what, to no avail.

NORM

Four?

MARK

Four. Four silver clit rings—that's what the ex had.

NORM

Pardon—What?

MARK

Yes! Not one! Not three!

NORM

—Not two.

MARK

Four! I'm like, damn, bitch! How many guys you plan on
fucking? 'Cause that kind of jewelry isn't for yourself, it's for
others to discover.

NORM

And also to mutilate such a sensitive area—

MARK

Right! Save some skin for Daddy! That's why Sabina's butterfly is so sexy. It's like discreet but enticing.

NORM

And it's located where Kundalini energy is stored.

MARK

What?

NORM

Kundalini energy. It's like an untapped universal power source.

MARK

Down there? What would that be, the power to blow water farts?

(*chuckles*)

NORM

Moving on…. When's the marriage?

MARK

We haven't set a date yet. Next year maybe? Whenever.

NORM

And how long ago did you say you met her?

MARK

Three—let me think—It'll be three weeks tomorrow.

NORM

Happy anniversary.

MARK

Thanks, man.... Sorry about that fart comment. Can you cut that part out?

NORM

I can.

CHAPTER 14

The sun has set and the party people have come out to play. There's the pull tabs lady doing her thing, getting the attention of some sort of man servant who brings her pull tab games at the sound of her caw.

The crowd is going wild with applause and I am frantically directing the camera man to follow the action, figuring it out as I go along.

Zoom out of the crowd applauding. Zip pan to the object of their affection: Ethel, queen of bingo, survivor of throat cancer, being rolled up to her special hydraulic throne. She is prim and proper befitting a lady of age. She even waves to the crowd in that stilted way European royals and Miss Americas do. But also, probably because of chronic pain in her joints.

Maybe somewhere in the melee I'll edit in grainy stock footage of an opossum being eaten from the inside by maggots on a hot paved road, or black and white shots of a little boy doing jumping jacks in a 1950s public service announcement. I can figure out the meaning later, I'm just thinking it will add that Oliver Stone element this thing desperately needs as a callback to when Mandy asked if I was the great director himself.

When the noise dies down from Ethel's grand entrance I yield my directorship to Mandy like she's second unit. I consider it a peace offering from when I told her not to direct. "Okay, walk us through this," I say.

She seems nervous but she's a pretty good narrator. "There's Ethel. All hail the queen. Over yonder way is the MC and his bingo balls. Let's go there—Have you seen that yet, the ah—?"

"Yeah, I can't. The powers that be are letting me film this under the conditions that I do not interview the MC and do not bother her highness, Ethel," I tell her.

"Did they say why?"

"Mine is not to question. Two small rules. Who cares anyway? This is about the people of bingo not the process."

"I suppose. But wouldn't it be cool to hear Ethel talk with a finger in her throat?"

"Kinda." And what I mean is, *absolutely.*

"I wonder if she fucks with that thing."

"Disgusting!" And what I mean is, *intriguing.*

"Throat fuck. It's all the rave." Boy, Mandy's on a roll. A tumble I dare not follow.

I verbally nudge her with, "Moving on...."

"*Throat Box: The Movie*! Starring Kevin Bacon as *Sticky Fingers Johnson*!"

"Moving on!"

"This film has not yet been rated."

At that I emphatically whistle the words *moving on* and she relents. As annoying as her humor is, I'm glad she's back in high spirits. Mandy is bubbly by nature. I like it better when she bubbles.

She says, "You know Marge. And there's Stanley over there...." She has no problem loudly pointing them out.

But suddenly she sees someone and in that seeing changes her demeanor to conciliatory. She whispers to the camera and it reminds me of how easily we anthropomorphize objects. I mean she's not doing that now, she's just whispering to the camera, like I said. But I'm thinking about robots. It's totally unrelated. My head isn't in the game at the moment. But robots aren't that far off. And we may have to play bingo with them someday, so it applies. Loosely.

Anyway, she whispers, "See the Latina lady there?— Do *not* talk to her."

"Why not?" I ask.

"No. Don't. She's a Puerto Rican chick with a couple of brats, lives on welfare, abusive husband—the whole nine yards."

"Who here hasn't used food stamps at the snack bar?" I ask this rhetorically. Because, *duh*.

"I'm warning you, if you include her in your masterpiece critics will call you a racist."

"That's silly!"

"No, she's a stereotype."

"But she's real!"

"You ever watch *Siskel & Ebert*?"

"When I couldn't sleep, yes.   Before the passing of Siskel."

"Ever notice how they loved all of Spike Lee's films? Ever notice how most of those films suck?"

"He has some decent movies," I reply.

"Some. But not all. My advice? Stay away. Stay far away."

I giggle. I think she's being funny even if she's not. I say, "Too late. We filmed her the other day. Onward, stripper soldier." And we move on.

She tries to grab the camera lens to pull us where she wants to go but the camera man rightly swats her away and she understands that there's no need to drag us. We will follow. Follow her to the end of the earth if need be.

Or to the snack bar, which is where we've arrived.

"Over here we have the snack booth full of sinful

goodies," she says.

She's treating this like a home movie. She doesn't know any better. It's precious. Like when little girls baby a doll. Although I guess they're supposed to do that 'cause usually the doll is a baby.

I chime in: "Someone recommended the jalapeño poppers."

Unconsciously, Mandy rubs her belly when she responds. "Eat at your own risk, my friend.... Oh, there's the kids from New York, did you get them yet?"

"Done. They claim to hate bingo," I confide.

"Sure they do. What metropolis-dwelling animals want to look like hicks? Bingo is for losers where they come from."

"But you want to be queen!"

"You calling me a loser?!"

I can't tell if she's joking or not. "I-I don't—I don't think so. You called me Jar-Jar!"

"Way to be defensive. Let's go to the smoking section." She cocks her head at the camera. "Ah. My people."

CUT TO:

BINGO PALACE - MEN'S BATHROOM CONFESSIONAL. RECORDED YESTERDAY.

We pick up with Jesse, the lone African-American man in the Bingo Palace who won a lucrative round.

NORM

Why are you so... excitable?

JESSE

Excitable? Is that what I am? Allow me to clue you in: while your granddaddy was telling you about us inferior niggers dangling from trees, my granddaddy was wiping his ass and telling me how kind and decent White folks are, if you just stay in line and keep your Black mouth shut!

NORM

So the burden is on you.

JESSE

Wake up, White boy! The burden never wasn't.

Brief pause.

NORM

Whew! I am feeling the burn! This is so new to me, this openness. So real!

101

JESSE
(*puts on a voice*)
Glad to wake yo ass up, suh! Dinnah be at six sharp, den
Mo'gan Freeman gonna drive you to da sto'!

CUT BACK

We're in the smoking section now. We're one glass wall away from being able to breathe normally. I imagine this is what purgatory feels like. Or Pompeii. Right before those lazy villagers became a sculpture garden.

Mandy has giddily traipsed us over to the table containing literally hundreds of different pull tab cards. We examine it thoroughly as the cameraman scans everything.

"Look at this." I am truly in awe. There's a whole business nobody gives a second thought to right here on this table. I mean some factory somewhere in Indonesia is right now slaving away—literally slaving away—its women and children to create a table of pull tab cards for American minimum wage slaves to yank open in the hopes of winning... something. I don't know what. That's why we have Mandy, thank God, to parse it out for us.

"Pull tabs for the true bingo junkie," Mandy says.

I ask, "What's the theory behind these?"

"The theory? Pull the tabs and you win. The catch is you usually win so little, you wind up spending your booty on more pull tabs in a never-ending cycle to hit the jackpot."

"It's a gambling vortex," I observe.

Mandy says, "It's all a gambling vortex—gambling is a vortex where the winner is the gal who breaks even."

"Yes, just like the dreaded tornado, gambling is hollow at the center."

"But if you can reach it you will be safe."

"Safe from the twister that is irony."

"I thought the twister was gambling?"

"Either way. Either way you appear profound," I playfully assure her.

"Thank you," she says.

And then it happens. I see the greatest thing that I have ever seen. I see what every documentary about a crumbling subculture needs: a train wreck of humanity.

There, sitting on the floor at the back of the room, obscured by the fog of exhaled smoke of a people murdering themselves with mild abandon are two young men dressed gothically. I don't mean just, like, in black—I mean *gothically*. *Renaissance festival* gothically. I mean *nerds*. Nerds who have encircled themselves with multicolored pebbles, no doubt lovingly smoothed in a rock tumbler, and burning incense. Jasmine-scented, I think. Or Celestial

Sandalwood. Because... you know... this place doesn't have enough smoke in the air.

I ask Mandy the only question that makes sense at this point: "For the love of all things Middle Earth, What. Is. *That?*"

"Where?"

Is she playing dumb? I don't want to point and stare, but I point. And stare. And spit, "There! How could I have missed that?"

"Oh, those two. Yeah, that's Bob The Mystic and his apprentice, Had Matter."

"This is too good to be true!"

She nonchalantly gestures for us to come with her. I guess she'll be making introductions on my behalf.

As we close in on movie magic, she warns us, "They're weird. Bob had this moment of enlightenment some years back after watching *Mazes & Monsters*."

"Right! Yeah, that old Tom Hanks flick!"

"Legend has it, after he saw that movie he wrote his own bible and brainwashed the Boy Wonder there. They changed their names, founded a two-man commune, and here they are—"

"—playing bingo," I finish for her. "I can't use this! This is a gold mine waiting to be discovered and no one's going to believe it."

You remember that scene in *Jurassic Park* where everyone looks up at the dinosaurs, slack-jawed? And then the other scene where they do that? And the other one? And the other one? You remember all the scenes where they do that? That's me. All of those in one right now. Plus the sequel.

I cannot wait for Mandy's introduction. I burst by her and exclaim, "Excuse me, gentlemen!"

I fully expect them to yell "Hark!" and "Who goes there?" Instead Bob the Mystic whispers something in Had Matter's ear and what I get is Had Matter telling me, "Bob The Mystic says, 'Good Evening.'"

I both ignore and embrace the unfolding awkwardness. It is like an epiphany, this moment. I now realize that my ability to embrace thus is one of the true gifts I've carried with me my whole, albeit short, adult life.

I say, "I see you are enjoying a game of bingo."

Again, Bob whispers in Had Matter's ear.

"Bob the Mystic says, 'Yes. Indeed we are.'" Had Matter states it in what I assume is his trademark monotone declarative voice.

"Does Bob the, ah, Bob The Mystic—does he talk at all, er...?"

My question is met with the unrelenting whisper routine. And then, "Bob the Mystic speaks only to the

Creator of All That Is Existence and Had Matter. You shall direct any and all questions through Had Matter." Make no mistake: this is still Had Matter telling me this.

"May I direct them through the Creator instead?" I ask.

After some whispering, which is growing weary in record time, Had Matter reveals, "Neither Bob The Mystic nor, by extension, Had Matter find that last question humorous. Contrary. They find it insulting."

"Sorry," I say.

Mandy tugs at my shirt. "Must be the shadow kicking in. I'm gonna play some bingo. Come get me when you're ready." She says that and walks away. I could have sworn she'd already walked away—I forgot all about her. That in itself is a magic trick. Such is the spell these two have cast upon me.

"Listen, I'm documenting the nightly ritual that is bingo. Do either of you have any insight into this meta-phenomenon? Perhaps this is how vampirism started?" I ask.

This time, no whispering. Had Matter dares to brave it alone: "Neither Bob the Mystic nor, by extension, Had Matter wish to comment on the issues of which—"

Bob gently but firmly but awkwardly but awesomely places his hand on Had Matter's heart, which silences him.

There is a pause and let me tell you, it. Is. *Dramatic.*

When Bob The Mystic deigns it proper to speak, his delivery is like that of a beat poet. He puts me in mind of the greats: Kerouac, Ginsberg, Farrakhan.

Bob The Mystic speaketh: "You have replaced ri-tu-al with sche-du-al. Instead of ex-er-cise by playing in the park, you jog around that great park calling upon the demons of headphone music and sun glasses to block out the pos-si-bi-li-ty of human interaction."

"What would the ancients say?" I can't tell who is more rhetorical or if either of us mean anything coming from our mouths. Another personal revelation. This is therapy for me. I love this guy already.

"You know, Norman—"

"How did you know my name?"

"—The Artist Formerly Known As Prince once sang a verse from a fine song called *Dolphin*, which asks why his brother has to starve when he was told there was a bounty of food. Furthermore, this is the man standing beside the man who stands ready to catch you should you fall."

Before I can conjure the significance, Had Matter breaks in softly with the chorus about coming back in the next life as a dolphin. Bob waves his hand in front of Had Matter's face like a magic wand. As if hypnotized, Had Matter bows his head in silence.

"That particular chorus is not applicable to the moral," Bob corrects. It doesn't sound chastising the way he says it but it's obvious that Had Matter knows he dun wrong.

"That's disappointing," I admit.

"Do not be that man, Norman. Do not be the starving one who stands next to the man. Be *the* man... Be *the* man...." And now Bob The Mystic, too, goes quiet. I think he's artfully persuading me to let it all sink in.

And it does. I say, "I think I have that album—Is that the one with *Pussy Control*?"

CHAPTER 15

We have a nice chat, me and the boys, director to magi. Speaking of M words, I need to find Mandy. She's the centerpiece after all. And my ride.

Oh, there she is, puffing away on a smoke, playing a game of skinny H. I cannot believe I'm learning the names of these games by sight. I'm starting to get why people do bingo night religiously.

I smooth Mandy's shoulder with a comforting hand so as not to startle her when me and the crew come up from behind. "You winning yet?" I ask.

"I'm on!" She's got that look of nervous anticipation like a sprinter at the starting line awaiting the shotgun.

"Describe that for us."

"On. It means I'm close to winning."

"Describe the feelings you are experiencing."

Before she can answer, the MC changes her feelings altogether when he says over the loudspeaker, "G-sixty."

A man at an adjacent table yells bingo and the crowd

sighs, "Awe!" One would hope they'd feel joy on his behalf.

"I feel like killing that fucker!" Mandy blurts reflexively.

"That's... that's valid."

CUT TO:

BINGO PALACE - MEN'S BATHROOM CONFESSIONAL. RECORDED YESTERDAY.

Sabina, Mark's better half by far, sits on the toilet confessional.

SABINA

The food's okay. People are kinda dorky. I don't know.... What else is there to do around here?

NORM

Any ambitions of moving back to the Big Apple?

SABINA

I want to but Mark wants to stay. He likes it here, it makes him feel superior.

NORM

Is that reason enough to uproot your life? Because your
fiancée has some ego issues?

SABINA

He's not my fiancée, we're just dating.

NORM

What? He said you were getting hitched.

SABINA

See any rings on these fingers? No, we haven't even
discussed it—I mean come on! We just met!

NORM

Well... I think you two have a lot to work out.

SABINA

Thanks, Dad. Naw, no marriage. I like men too much. I need
to experience more of life first before I settle down.

NORM

So you left New York because...?

SABINA

I don't know, change of pace?

NORM

That can be therapeutic.

SABINA

Mmm. Maybe I'll fuck my way back to Brooklyn.

NORM

Excuse me?!

SABINA

Kidding! I'm kidding.

NORM

Tell us: Where does Sabina see herself in ten years?

SABINA

Not here playing bingo that's for damn sure! No... Um... I
don't know I haven't given it much thought. You think Mark
and I will last?

Long dead silence.

CUT BACK

This is tense. It hasn't even started yet and I can feel the electricity in the air. That could also be the wiring in this place. There's enough EMF in the room to trap a ghost. But something less *sciencey* than that tells me I'm in for a dizzying ride.

"What are we playing here?" I ask.

"Speed bingo. Get ready," Mandy says, eyes trained on her spread of cards.

I've only got one card. But still, "I don't know about this!"

Speed bingo is as it sounds. That's the beauty of everything here, it is all as it sounds. It's only frustrating when you realize you're locked into a chunk of time where you cannot ask questions for the film you're shooting because you've got to stamp out lettered numbers on paper with your dye blotter if you want to have a prayer of winning a couple hundred bucks. And because everyone around you is also praying and playing for that couple hundred bucks, you can't ask them questions anyway without rousing their ire. Neither can you pray, for God is busy answering them. Mainly, with disappointment. As is His wont. No judgements here.

But, since we are filming every last thing, this might be a good spot for a montage where we see in quick succession Mandy's delight and my frustration, the reactions of those around us, Mandy and I playfully nudging each other, and other such happy affairs enacted during these six rounds of speed bingo.

The clips would be short, but, I'm thinking, in slow motion with a feel-good soundtrack over them. Something Beach Boys if I can afford it. Something Beach Boys-ish if I can't. And above all this bustle you'll hear... my voice over... smooth, like silver bells....

NORM (VOICE OVER)

Sharing. Searching. Loving. Speed bingo. I didn't have what it took to win and that was okay by me. Playing with Mandy that night was the guiltiest pleasure I've known since I jumped into the shark tank at Sea World. I was six then. Now I'm twenty-five. Things have changed. For one thing, I'm twenty-five. For another, I've experienced the sheer horror of speed bingo with a new friend. If I had to do it all over again I wouldn't change a thing. Except I might not jump into a shark tank at Sea World. And I wouldn't play speed bingo ever.

And then we'll cut back into the scene to about where we are now, with the MC alerting us of intermission.

***

Patrons are stretching, many in stretch pants, whether they bought them that way or not, and shuffling about like Romero's directing.

Mandy looks at me. Really looks into me for the first time in a long time. "That was fun," she says. I can tell she's exhilarated. Me? I'm exhausted.

"Yeah. Not only did I lose the game, I lost some... I lost some vision, too. You actually like that? You look fuzzy," I half joke.

"Love it. It's my favorite game," she says.

"Wow. Your powers of concentration are nothing short of astounding." I didn't think it would be possible to be impressed by bingo skills, but color me thus.

Mandy flashes her wad of green and says, "Two hundred bucks, easy money!"

"So who all won? You won twice and that guy won one."

She says, "Someone in nonsmoking won."

"But Ethel won twice."

"Don't rub it in."

"I'm not, I'm *Scoobie-Doo*-ing. How could a woman that infirm win speed bingo not once but twice when I couldn't even keep up?"

"This is your first time playing. Ethel has bingo

running through her veins and she also has a nurse."

"So?"

"Four eyes are better than two."

"I used to say that in middle school but no one bought it." I laugh alone on that one. For a little too long, maybe. I figure if I keep laughing she'll laugh. I figure wrong.

She says, "Bet you got your ass kicked a lot in school, huh?"

"No!"

"Yes you did!"

"No! Shut up!"

"Ahh...?"

Like a middle school boy I blurt, "Not by girls!"

I like that she's comfortable taunting me. It's fun. I think she's starting to dig me, which could wind up a problem if things get too serious between us. Gotta keep that professional boundary up. Gotta remind myself this is how The Beatles broke up.

CHAPTER 16

Mandy's about to go potty and I'm about to Windex the handicap stall in the men's room so we can set up a new confessional. I'll never understand these little coves where the bathrooms are. They're not long enough to be hallways. They're just a way to section off poop noises from the burping, farting, talking in the main hall. There's sometimes a water bubbler in them, though not this one.

Here in the Bingo Palace's poop cove we're blessed with a payphone and I'm blessed with some dude on it. Mercifully, he's not so loud that "Boom Mic" Mike can't angle him down to a whisper. But he's still in the shot. He better not pull focus if we need to use this footage.

"You definitely cannot follow me into this bathroom, folks." Mandy says this to the camera then pushes on the stained wooden door. I mean *stained* in both ways.

I ask, "Want anything from the snack bar?"

"No thanks," she says.

"Poppers, cheese fries... anything?" I offer again.

Maybe she doesn't get that I'm buying.

"Nope. Help yourself." And then she leaves us.

In the absence of her noise the dude on the phone sounds loud. He says to whoever he's talking to, "No, we need you down here! Too many people—" Then he notices the camera for the first time and conceals his conversation with his hand, but it's still not as muffled as he'd like. I, however, have zero interest in spying on him, so I gesture for "Boom Mic" Mike and the camera guy to follow me to get some poppers. I hope there's more jalapeño and cheese to them than crusty shell. But I also hope they aren't soggy. I hope that more. I'll take either. I'll likely get neither.

"Too many legit wins. They're afraid," the stranger attempts to whisper. And then he yells, "Because there's a camera!" I take that as my cue to swing the camera back around. Poppers can wait.

I eyeball him a sec. He says, "Hey," his eyes alternately addressing me and the camera in nervous fluctuations.

"How are you?" I ask.

"You mind if I get some privacy?" he says.

"Say no more!"

The man goes back to his phone conversation. I subtly signal to my crew not to take us off of him. I totally just ninja-ed this guy because he's talking at full volume as if we'd disappeared simply by the power of suggestion.

Frustrated about something, he barks, "I gotta go. Do your best—and bring Chuck if you find him!" into the receiver. Then he slams the pay phone down hard on its base and when he does is startled to find us standing behind him.

"You sound distraught," I state calmly.

With a terse "Excuse me" he gruffly walks through us.

I call after him asking if he needs to talk about it. I tell him I'm doing shadow work. I tell him the handicap stall will be open for business in 20 minutes if he changes his mind. I'm speaking to myself.

Poppers!

CHAPTER 17

"You sure you can handle this equipment?" I ask. Greasy flecks of popper spray out my mouth but I don't think I hit anyone so I'm not embarrassed. Mandy should be embarrassed—look at her there swinging the camera around like she's playing Superman with a toddler on her shoulder.

"I got it covered, eat your poppers. I'll interview you, it'll be fun," she says. I do as directed. When it comes to batter-fried anything with cheese, I can take direction like a certain Irish mayor of a certain fast food franchise that shall remain nameless. (Hint: It's not Supermac's.)

"So Norm, if you could make any movie what would it be?"

The camera is trained on me and I am trained alternately on my snacks and on Mandy's forehead just above the camera lens. That's always a good place to lock your eyes so as not to stare into the camera. All of this is just horseplay, though. I can't use any of it as I refuse to be in this film. I hate when filmmakers pull focus to concentrate on themselves. Some documentaries are about the subjects they claim to be about and some are about narcissism coated and fried in cheese. This one will have both if I use any of this footage.

I should have instructed the camera guy to pull the tape out before handing off to Mandy, like in every dumb movie where the gunslinger gives a gun with no bullets to the overeager dope who also wants a gun. Not that Mandy's a dope. I wonder if she owns a gun?

To her question I answer, "One that's already made or like my dream movie?"

"Yeah, one that's made—Your dream movie, you doof!"

"My dream was to do a buddy—like a buddy road picture with Bruce Campbell and Jim Carrey and Chris Farley. But Chris passed away and I've... dealt with that. There was some grieving, some denial... but basically, ah, I'm at peace with it."

"Uh-huh."

"We still have Costas Mandalor."

"Has working on this project helped you at all find yourself? Or confront your darker potentials?"

"Wow, that's a loaded one. Only time will tell," I say. I'm all but done with my deep frieds.

"What do you think—"

"But I do feel this will have been an utter failure if it does not."

"Uh-huh."

"I'm sorry, what were you about to ask?" Now's my chance to slurp on the soda cubes making bland water in my waxy cup.

"Oh no, I was just going to ask what you thought about the Smokers Conspiracy?"

I shrug it off. "It's just something to ask about, see if I can start a whole new paranoia."

Mandy says, "That's not very nice," like she means it.

"Even God envies the devil sometimes," I remind her. Or tell her. Maybe she never knew that.

"Good friends with God are ya?"

"Let's just say I'm in tune with my higher power and leave it at that."

"Yeah. Do you ever hear voices that tell you to kill?"

"Not 'til recently. Shall we wrap this thing up?"

I'm done eating. Time is money. So is tape. Yada-yada. Mainly I'm getting antsy to interview Bob The Mystic. There's a handicap stall with our name on it. Who knows when or if he'll leave this place? It's possible he lives here in these walls like the Phantom of The Bingo Palace.

Did I say *possible*? I meant *probable*.

Mandy says, "Saving the best for last... Norm

Plumber, you just made a docudrama. What are you gonna call it?"

"This movie?"

She nods the camera *yes*.

I say, "Oddly enough, *The Smokers Conspiracy*. How funny is that?"

"I knew it! That's exactly what I'd call it!"

"It is?"

"Of course! It's thematic—It pulls the picture together!"

"I know what *thematic* means."

"Brilliant minds think alike!" she says.

I smile in response. Weakly, but it's there. And she hands the camera back to the camera man without turning it off. I'd complain that this was time wasted, but really... come on.

CUT TO:

BINGO PALACE - MEN'S BATHROOM CONFESSIONAL. RECORDED TODAY.

BOB THE MYSTIC

Bin-go is ri-tu-al; bin-go is beau-ti-ful.

NORM

Define beauty.

BOB THE MYSTIC

Hu-manity has replaced beau-ty with vani...ty? ... They have
done so because they have destroyed the beauty of the earth
upon which they so carelessly graze. So now they have
turned to and against the very last image of beauty they
have: the one that lives backwards in the mirror. And since
they are made in God's image, and since they realize their
awesome ability to destroy all else God has created, they
have no need for God. Or God's image.

NORM

So they—we—destroy ourselves.

BOB THE MYSTIC

Anorexia; bulimia; heroin chic.

NORM

—Breast implants; Hanson....

BOB THE MYSTIC

Yes. A totally decimated picture of Woman since the days
when Man had Nature to pick apart.

NORM

And what about Man?

BOB THE MYSTIC

Ultimately Man is in control of image. When Man is through
with Woman he will turn on himself.

NORM

Wow! This is some overwhelming stuff, Bob The Mystic.

BOB THE MYSTIC

Knowledge is power, Norman. That is the first rule of the
Dungeon Master.

NORM

No question. How different would your life be if instead of
Mazes & Monsters, you had seen *The Leprechaun*?

BOB THE MYSTIC

Bob The Mystic cannot answer as he no longer views films.

NORM

What about *The Stuff*?

BOB THE MYSTIC

Bob The Mystic cannot answer as he no longer—

NORM

C.H.U.D.?

No response.

NORM (CONT' D)

C.H.U.D.?

BOB THE MYSTIC

Bob The Mystic has seen *C.H.U.D.*.

NORM

And?

Short pause. Bob winces.

BOB

Cannibalistic Humanoid Underground Dwellers.

NORM

And?

Short pause. Clearly it pains Bob to think about the
ramifications of C.H.U.D..

BOB THE MYSTIC
That is not the purpose for which film was invented!

NORM
No shit! Phew! I got scared for a minute there! Thought we'd
lost you for good!

CUT TO:

Mandy was kind enough and patient enough to make small talk with her bingoholic comrades while I wrapped up my bathroom stall confessionals. Now we're sitting in her car in the parking lot debating our next location shoot.

"Where to?" I ask.

"IHOP," she says.

"I'm not very hungry," I say.

"Good, you can watch me eat."

IHOP it shall be. I guess this is what people mean when they say *fair is fair*. Plus, she's driving.

CHAPTER 18

I always liked IHOP as an acronym because International House of Pancakes sounds so hoity-toity. IHOP sounds more like a bunny heading to the hopper after eating a Rooty Tooty Fresh 'N Fruity short stack. Speaking of which, Mandy is chowing down said trademarked pancakes right now. I'm sneaking a piece of her toast. Nothing better than hot buttery toast at night. Except in the morning. And again at noon. Toast is the best invention since sliced bread.

There is only one other customer in the joint: an old man sitting at the bar. Unless my eyes are deceiving me, he's sporting what looks to be a yarmulke with a swastika embroidered on top. And if you think I'm leaving here without interviewing that gent, you're as out of your mind as he is.

"See? Flapjacks. Tops off the night." Oh, right. Mandy. On with the show.

"Syrupy," I say, trying to look interested. I don't

know how long I can stave off my need to interview that man.

"Mmm! Everyone loves sap!" she enthuses.

"But cheese fries are gross," I say, calling out her hypocrisy.

"This isn't grease, it comes from bees."

"Honey."

"Hmm?"

"Honey comes from bees. Sap comes from trees." Don't know why I'm bothering. Neither of us is paying attention to the other.

"Bees; trees; dog fleas," she giggles. "Oh I must be tired!"

"You get the giggles when you're tired?" I ask.

"Big time. And I get the stupids, too."

"Dumber as the night goes on."

"You know it, baby. Must be the blonde in me."

"Are you smarter as a brunette?"

Mandy twirls her hair and says, "Yeah. And when I dye it red I get pissed off and drunk." She laughs, but I see something else in there. And *that* regains my interest.

I ask, "Do you like who you are?"

And she blurts, "Hello!"

"Too left field?"

"Smidgeon... Yeah, I guess I do. Does anyone? I think

it's a process of becoming and I like who I'm becoming: queen of all things bingo."

"I don't think that's what you want," I observe.

"What do I want?"

"I don't know but sometimes I get the feeling you're lying about the whole bingo thing, 'cause you make fun of it and stuff."

She contemplates thoughtfully a moment while flicking the straw of her orange juice for no conscious reason. Finally, "Not really. Not any more than anything else, it's just that I sense the negativity from you and then I feel stupid about my goals."

"Negativity? All right. So before I came along—"

"Norm I am one hundred percent certain of what I want. But that doesn't mean I'm blind to the fact that you think I'm a small town idiot."

"I don't think that! Why does everybody think I think that?" Seriously—why?

"You could. And that would be fine. I mean my defenses are up now but that's just self-preservation. When all the lights and cameras are gone and you're done scrutinizing my passion, I'm going to keep my life intact because no matter what it looks like to you—and to you out there in big screen land—I am at a place of peace far, far away from where I was even a year ago. You deserve your sliver of fame and I deserve mine. Same goal, different medium."

"You think I'm doing this for fame?"

"I know you're doing it for fame."

"I'm not doing anything for fame. If it happens, it's just incidental."

"You're making a movie. Fame is not incidental."

"Wha—? This isn't *Bicycle Thief* o r—o r *Space Truckers*!"

She looks away and concedes, "You're right," then looks directly into my eyes and in all seriousness continues, "Now who's the idiot?"

SLOW DISSOLVE TO:

INSERT - BINGO PALACE - MEN'S BATHROOM
CONFESSIONAL. RECORDED TODAY.

Had Matter looks like he's in deep contemplation, seriously straining to answer a question we never hear asked. After some time he opens his mouth to speak, but before sound can escape....

CUT BACK TO SCENE:

"Still you! If you think my take on the bingo scene is hostile that's your own perception! I came into this thing with no preconceived notions and I think—or at least I've tried to keep that same level of objectivity," I say. I'll admit I'm a bit perturbed.

Like she's toying with me she responds, "So you haven't met any morons since you started? Nothing about this turns you off?"

"How can you ask that about your would-be subjects, queeny?"

"Because there *are* a lot of morons, Norm. And I will rule them. They will applaud when I enter the building like I'm a fat old Elvis. But there are also decent people. Struggling people. All walks of people."

"I treat everyone with the same sense of dignity."

"Then why after all your little reality TV intimate chats is the buzz still about how you're planning on taking us down?"

I have no idea what she just said. "I have no idea what you just said."

"Documentary or mockumentary? That is the question."

"Thrillomedy—Remember that word?"

"That's your answer?"

"No. This *is* what it *is*, that's all. I don't want to take anyone down, that's silly. I wouldn't even know how to go about doing something like that. Just by poking fun at you? —What? 'Cause I'm not even attempting to do that," I explain.

She says, "Huh." And then is happy go lucky all of a sudden. "Okay, just wondering!"

She shrugs it off and is all over that straw, slurping away at the bottom of her empty OJ glass like a child.

"You're okay?" I ask.

"Fine! Just wanted to make sure we're on the same team!"

"Oh. You could have just asked."

"I did."

"Right. You have some valid concerns." I'm fishing now, I just don't know for what for.

She says, "I know. You wanna blow this popsicle stand?"

"Are we following you home?" I ask.

"It's up to you if you need the footage."

"Let's do it."

* * *

While Mandy's at the front waiting for a cashier to emerge from the kitchen so she can pay her bill with my money, the crew and I swoop in on the old man in the strange yarmulke. Because this. Has. To. Happen.

As respectfully as one can, given that one (this one) has just shoved a camera in some elderly stranger's face, I say, "I don't mean to disturb you sir, but I couldn't help noticing your headdress. Do you play bingo?"

The old man waves it off with an "Aaaaah." As in *Aaaah, I don't play that crap.*

"Have you ever?" I ask.

"Once? Twice, maybe?—In the past. I like cribbage," he tells me.

"Great, you qualify. What's the story behind the yarmulke? Are you Jewish?"

"If I were not, why would I put myself through the persecution of the Chosen People?"

"Social experiment? I have no answers."

"You want to know about the swastika," he guesses.

"Exactamundo."

"Swastika was a Kabbalistic solar symbol used to contemplate the cyclical nature of life before Hitler stole it from us. So I stole it back, end of story."

"That's an amazing idea."

"Not so. The Blacks destroyed the word n*egro* and took ownership of the word *nigger*. Now they're African Americans—and in a span of about twelve years! Now *that's* amazing!"

"I never really thought about it that way."

"No. That's the problem with your generation. You got no reason to think. Pretty soon dreams will be literal translations of the previous day!"

"That would suck."

"Yes it would! It would! ... What is this with the lights and the camera?"

"I'm making a documentary about bingo."

"Oh. Big demand for a movie about bingo, is there?"

"The demand creates itself," I explain.

"Nothing creates itself! Except God—and even He needs help sometimes! You know back in my youth I was a street musician in London. Played violin. One day, a man approaches me. He listens to me play for quite some time but never tosses me a penny. Well, he sees my look of greedy disappointment and says, 'You don't play for this... you play for this.' And he taps my donations jar and violin respectively. Then he says, 'When you're worth money, you won't need this,' referring to the jar. He put me on the floor with that comment. And do you know who that man was?"

I indicate that I do not, because... I do not.

"P.D.Q. Bach," he reveals. "Really! P.D.Q. Bach! The key is, stay true to your art and true to yourself. The rest comes naturally. Or in my case, not. As it turns out I'm a train wreck of a violinist! What can I do?"

I sit with that a moment to really take in what he's telling me here. "So you think I'm a jackass, too."

"What?"

"Nothing."

CUT TO:

BINGO PALACE - MEN'S BATHROOM CONFESSIONAL. RECORDED TODAY.

HAD MATTER
Bingo is ri-tu-al; bingo is beau-ti-ful.

NORM
I asked Bob The Mystic to define beauty but I wasn't concise. So I ask you: Bingo is beautiful. What does that mean?

HAD MATTER
Humanity has replaced beauty with vanity.

NORM
Yeah, that's the part I got from him.

HAD MATTER

Then that is the answer you seek.

NORM

Gotcha. Now the name "Had Matter." Where does that come from?

No response.

NORM (CONT'D)

Pare—ah—parents? Parents?

No response.

NORM (CONT'D)

The average Joe would probably guess that it is a play on the fictitious character, "Mad Hatter" from *Alice In Wonderland*. But I'm going to go out on a limb here, with zero judgements in my heart, and say its true meaning is that before you met Bob The Mystic, you used to matter but now you don't have an original thought in your head. How close am I?

Dramatic pause. Had Matter finds his center.

HAD MATTER

At its core, thought, not matter, composes the material universe. The internalization of this basic truth shall be the next leap in human evolution. Therein lies meaning.

NORM

Says Bob The Mystic.

HAD MATTER

Yes.

NORM

So then at its core, I was right about your name.

CHAPTER 19

I am standing in Mandy's doorway with my trusty film crew for what is probably the last time. We will keep in touch I am sure. But we will not get too close. You never want to get too close to your subject. Documenting has that in common with stripping. Maybe that's why we gravitated toward each other when we first met those many hours ago. Feels like years. I feel like I've grown up with this woman.

"This is goodbye," I say. I go in for the farewell hug. I've never hugged a woman with fake breasts before. Her chest feels like the playpen at Chuck E. Cheese's.

Mandy is buoyant. And *buoyant*. "This is goodnight," she tells me more than the camera. And her hug is heartfelt, I can tell that. She wants to stay in contact. Maybe even date me. We've been through a lot together in a little time. We are a living montage.

"What is next for Mandy-Alise?" I ask.

She says, "You could do like a *60 Minutes* thing where you check up on me in a few years."

"Neither the budget nor the impetus, Mandy. Mandy-Banandy." I laugh at my wordplay. Somebody has to—

"Cute. Real original." —because she won't.

I rhetorically tell her *I try* and she moves on to, "Whelp, love her or hate her, the clock is ticking on dear old Ethel."

"Yes. It's as if the Fates had an extra spool of thread lying around."

That she laughs at then says, "Yeah, too bad they couldn't sew that throat back up!" And here she guffaws, but it turns to a somber realization midstream. "That was rude," she admits, rebuking herself.

"It's okay."

"No. I shouldn't have said that."

"You're tired."

"Yeah, run down."

"Any final thoughts before we throw in the towel?" I ask.

She thinks hard enough for lines to crinkle her forehead. Finally, "Not at the moment."

"Last call on the moment. Going once... going twice...."

Mandy turns to the camera. "Bingo rules." She flashes the peace sign.

I say, "There you go," and call cut. That's a wrap.
Or so I think.

CHAPTER 20

Many are the nights spent secluded in my bedroom on my iMac editing this beast into a movie. I think doing a documentary is like chiseling at stone until the sculpture forms. By the end I figure I'll have an eye-opening, if instructive, documentary. The kind of film middle school health teachers will force trapped students to watch on a chipped green projector, dusty and hairy, antiquated by 1980s standards. Yeah, you remember those? *Don't be a Johnny Don't. Be a Johnny Do.*

But now—just now—the totally unexpected is happening and this Johnny Don't Johnny *did*. Did find something he's playing over and over again to make sure it's real. He, *me*. I'm doing this, I mean.

Three months into editing my first feature film and it's time to pick up the camera again. I can't believe this. It's time to film the ending I never saw coming.

"THREE MONTHS LATER...."

INTERIOR - NORM'S APARTMENT - DAY

Norm dials his phone. Mandy's answering machine picks up on the other end.

MANDY (ANSWERING MACHINE)
Hello. You have reached Mandy-Alise. Or her machine at least. Hey, that rhymes! Anywho, leave it at the beep!
(*a beat; quickly*)
I drive a jeep!

The machine BEEPS.

NORM
Hi. Yeah, ah, hi. It's Norm. Plumber. Remember me? I was the cute affable guy with the—

We hear FEEDBACK as Mandy PICKS UP on the other end.

MANDY (OFF CAMERA)
Norm?

NORM
Yeah! Hi!

MANDY (O.C.)

Hold on. Let me shut this thing off.

She does so. The feedback STOPS.

MANDY (O.C.) (CONT'D)

Can you hear me now?

NORM

Loud and clear.

MANDY (O.C.)

Oh my god! How are you? How's the film?

NORM

Good. How's... burgers?

MANDY (O.C.)

Burgers?

NORM

Flipping burgers?

MANDY (O.C.)

Oh, I gave that up a month ago. I went back to stripping.

NORM
Good for you.

MANDY (O.C.)
Yeah, more money.

NORM
Right; right. Listen, I need to see you if that's possible. There's something I have to show you. When can I come by?

CHAPTER 21

God, do I ever love a good frosty beverage. It can be anything, almost. But I especially love root beer. I'm not drinking root beer now, just mentioning it. Now I'm drinking Juicy Juice. Not sure which flavor. Vomit, I think.

"What's so important you have to show me?"

Mandy looks a little nervous but it's me slightly bouncing up and down on her love seat, frosty mug cupped in two hands, staring off into what I wish was a fireplace but is really the blank screen of her television.

"Mmm! Right. Have a seat," I say, remembering why I'm here. With the crew. Filming.

"My place, but thanks," she shoots.

I look at her like, *Mind if I...?* and jiggle a videotape at her. She gestures *Be my guest*, so I pop it into her VCR and turn on the TV. I turn around and look up at her hovering, arm-folded form. God, those breasts are like shelves. Puffy, awesome shelves.

"Have a seat," I tell her again. She throws her hands

up like, *This better be good,* and says, "All righty." Then she plops down where I just was and I know I have both her attention and her annoyance.

I stand. I address. "When I was editing this puppy, something strange caught my eye. At first I thought I was going nuts but then you add it together and... well.... How's the board game, hmm?"

I cave because I'm nervous.

"Norm...?"

"Sexecutioner's Noose, right? Any buyers?"

"Selling like hot cakes—What are you stalling for?"

Solemnly, I press the green PLAY triangle on the VCR. Show, don't tell. That's for what film is for, right?

And there it is for all the world to see. Or Mandy, at least. My Zapruder film; my back and to the left, back and to the left. Together we watch clips of scenes that felt innocent enough when we shot them. Strung together, they show a clear system of signals controlled by Ethel wherein she chooses who wins and who loses bingo.

It's the darndest setup. Ethel's... how do I put this delicately? Her bag of colostomy juice bubbles out a type of morse code, which then gets interpreted by that woman I thought was crazy who just says "Pull tabs" all night. She says her catch phrase and the man who pulls the balls from the bingo cage extrapolates meaning from the rate at which she blurts those two syllables.

The point is made. I pause the tape.

"The Smokers Conspiracy lives. What is going through your mind right now?" I ask Mandy.

"Oh. Oh, is this part of the documentary? This is where you gage my reaction to a bunch of bullshit you pasted together in a meaningful way? Fuck you, Norm! Everyone was right about you!"

"I thought you might react adversely. But I'm not offended because it's not my imagination. Okay, now brace yourself. This part's the kicker...."

Hovering over the TV, I press play on the magic wand that is her VCR remote control. Onscreen pops the scene by the bathrooms where Mandy goes to do her business and we ended up cueing in on that stranger's phone call at the payphone. Remember that? Well, it turns out he's not just any stranger. He's the guy who works the bingo ball cage.

"I cut out the foreground and turned up the volume on the background so you can hear. It's coming up...." I prep her.

Too many legit wins... They're afraid.... Because there's a camera!

I looped the clip for emphasis so that we can watch it over and over again. Back and to the left, back and to the left.

The footage cuts out. I eject the VHS tape and turn off the TV in two jerks of the remote. I am a master of my domain even in Mandy's domain.

"That's it," I say with a tight grin of both satisfaction and concern.

"That's it? That's my life you're fucking with, Norm. What do you expect me to do with this? Turn them in? Shut the place down? Forget my dreams, huh? Why are you doing this? Because I won't sleep with you or because you think I'm pathetic? You like to pull wings off of flies, Norm, that's what this is. And you can justify it anyway you want but you're fucking laughing on the inside, deep down where you don't even feel it."

"I'm sorry. I know this is difficult." I move to console her where she sits but she has other plans. Plans that involve bolting up and shoving us out her front door like evil astronauts from an airlock.

"You don't know dick! You got what you wanted now. Now just... Go. Away," she says.

My feet fumble backwards into her little hallway nook, but it's my words that are really tripping. "This isn't what I.... This isn't.... I thought you'd want to.... I dunno. There are no words."

"There are no words, Norman. Wait, here's a few....

Go? Yes. Go fuck yourself."

"Well, whatever you decide, good luck. I really am sorry it's ending this way," I tell her. And I mean it no matter what she thinks.

"Tell it to the shadow." She slams the door in my face. The crew do a good job staying over my shoulder, capturing everything. I've lost her. But we've captured her, too. It's surreal, yet it's nothing compared to what happens next.

CHAPTER 22

Through a lighted mist the white of purity, the white of death, a seemingly disembodied hand in a loose-fitted robe cracks gavel to coaster. A face leans in from the mist: a caucasian woman. Salt and pepper hair with graying sides. Angular bifocals. Furrowed brow. Disdain and spittle flying from her jawing mouth, but we don't hear what she's saying. This is a judge in her courtroom. This is the face of justice.

This is how I imagine the prelude to me opening the letter I hold in my hand would go had I the budget to execute a reenactment. Instead I'll just open the letter and read highlights....

"Dear Sir:

The damage you have caused our community is immense. You have no idea what you've done. I must speak with you at once. Meet me in the smoking section of the palace. Door will be open. No cameras. Come alone."

And now picture me glancing away pensively from the letter in closeup, like Clark Kent about to solve a riddle and go all Superman on Calvin Denby. We'll dissolve to a montage of newspaper clippings from trial. *The* trial.

Did I mention the trial?

In the end Mandy did the right thing. I accidentally left the tape in her VCR. Unless there are no accidents and it was fate. Not sure where I fall on that one where this is concerned but in either event, she passed it on to the Gaming Commission—and not anonymously, either.

The scandal broke in all the local papers. Her story was read by local yokels for miles around, right there on page B-eight underneath the Horoscope Section. Or perhaps page B-eleven, wedged between lingerie and used car dealership adverts.

One thing is certain: The Bingo Palace won't be calling out B-eight or B-eleven anytime soon. If they ever do get their license reinstated, I'm sure they'll have a new bingo queen. The true bingo queen. Mandy-Alise.

CHAPTER 23

What happens next is a true *show, don't tell.* For this I will require a reenactment with either actors who will work for screen credit or maybe the real people who, though they loathe me now, are pretty freed up time-wise.

What follows really did happen, though, to the best of my recollection. I wasn't allowed to bring a camera crew so we can go crazy and rent a crane—or... well... a jib—and fake the swooping Scorsese shots. This will be added value and look awesome in the final cut.

INTERIOR - BINGO PALACE/SMOKING SECTION - DAY

I enter the now-abandoned Bingo Palace. Swoop goes the camera! (Just pretend.) The stuffy decay of cigarettes and people sweat... it smells like the between-rounds panting of a hobo fighter in here.

There, in the middle of the smoking section waits Ethel and

her nurse. Swoop!

We hear my feet pattering on the floor of the hall. And then I arrive. I stand before her. An eerie silence permeates the place. This is the moment in the *BAD* short film just after superhero Michael Jackson with his buckles and his breathing and his teased-out hair drops down from the ceiling of the New York subway and a steam pipe bursts— right at the moment when Wesley Snipes steps forward to say, "So what's up?" Spectacular moment. I'm nervous reliving it.

NORM

You know my lawyer would kill me if he saw me talking to you.

Ethel gives me the once-over. Slowly, angrily, she inserts her Nurse's thumb into her throat hole. For the first time, we hear her speak. Glorious.

ETHEL

So you're the puss toot what done shut down my Bingo Palace.

NORM

Sorry I missed the trial. I was out of the country that day.
From what I read, the joint closing had more to do with the
con job you guys were pulling than anything I did.

ETHEL
(*enunciates the g in "bologna"*)
Bologna! We performed a community service!

NORM
What service?—You steered the flow of money straight into
the pockets of your smoking buddies at the expense of—

ETHEL
No! No! Wrong! I have throat cancer! I'm dying of old age
and I can't even enjoy it! Luckily it's keeping me out of jail!

NORM
You take your good with your bad.

ETHEL
Shut up! Cancer is no joke! All those smokers who
participated in our so-called scam were trying to quit! One
quarter of the money earned went to their recovery and the
remainder was donated to cancer research! That is the scam
you exposed!

NORM

I didn't expose anything, lady.

ETHEL

It was your footage! Your camera!

NORM

Yes. And you would have gotten away with it if it wasn't for us meddling kids. I know I'm supposed to feel something about this, I just don't know what. You have cancer?—You're old! You earned money for a humanitarian cause?—Wrong! You stole it! I can't set the record straight on that! You pled your case and lost. You have an obsession. Go to therapy! It can be very therapeutic! As for me?—Fuck you!

(lateral lisp disappears)

I tried to do a balanced documentary on people I'd never want to be on your best day! I even offered to help some of you mother-fuckers out of your personal comas—but you wouldn't hear of it! You don't want help, you want to bitch! Mandy hates my guts—This whole town wants to shoot me! And now you, of all people, *you* expect me to justify your theft in the court of public opinion?! Well that's just dandy! I'll throw some flute and soft piano underneath your tearful confession, then we'll all feel for you. Yeah, why don't I

just.... Why don't I just jump off a fucking barn roof, you
horse! Moo!—Moo!
(*brays like a horse*)
God!
(*a beat; screams*)
Everything's going all wrong and I can't stand it!

The silence is oppressive. I catch my breath. It just got real. I
just mooed. Wrong animal. I'm not feeling myself.

ETHEL
What happened to your speech impediment?

NORM
What?!

ETHEL
Your speech impediment. Where did it go?

NORM
(*utterly shocked*)
What? Oh my god. Oh. My. God. *Ohmigod!!!* I-I-I feel...
cleansed! Like a huge block has been lifted off my chest!

ETHEL

157

Peachy. What about *my* pain?!

NORM

This is so F-ed up! I don't care about your pain. I never did!
I mean, I tried! But I couldn't care less! I really couldn't care
less! Ethel... Mrs. Ethel—whatever your name is—this is the
best thing that's ever happened to me! ... Thank you!

ETHEL

(*to nurse*)
I don't get it. What's happening here?

Her nurse shrugs, equally confused.

NORM

I lost my lateral lisp. Do you know how long I've had this
fucking thing? All my life! Do you have any idea how long
that is?!—Ha! ... Haaa!!!

My yell bounces off the walls. Great acoustics in here—at
least for the reenactment.

ETHEL

I'll be happy for you when I can walk again. Or talk like a
human.

NORM

No. You won't. You're miserable. You're all miserable! I may
have exposed your crimes but that's—those are just
projections of what's going on inside you. And for once in
my life, I can't help you, you.... So thank you! Fuck you. Fuck
you and goodnight.

I exit. No, more than that, I swoop away and ignore her life.
Ethel's colostomy bag bubbles in disdain. We hear my
voiceover from the present day.

PRESENT DAY NORM (VOICE OVER)

So this is who I am. The good. The bad. The wildly
inappropriate. This is who I am. Let 'em have their fifteen
minutes of fame and their day in court. Hoorah. For the first
time ever I get to be all of me. And that's far more
important. Of course you'd hate to have been the next
person I met because... well... gazing into the mirror at that
backwards reflection that searches me with his devil's smirk,
I knew then, as I still do, only one immutable truth: *Man,*
I'm a prick!

FADE OUT

CHAPTER 24

And so it is, and so I am, and so it shall be. Don't know if that makes sense but it feels like a wrap to a monumental story in the future history of cinema.

Oh, one more thing before we roll credits. I'm not lying when I say I didn't expose them. My footage didn't show a series of signals. Consciously, I thought it did, which is why I brought it to Mandy. Unconsciously, I made it up so I had a reason to see Mandy again.

Boobs. And she's a good person.

We could have been great together, but that's not the point. The point is, we both thought the footage was an accurate depiction of the scam and so she reported it. Ethel and her confederacy of dunces copped to it before they even reviewed the footage.

Turns out that although I was wrong, I was right. There really was a scam going on, just a little more altruistic than seedy. Oops.

To quote the late, great Alfred Hitchcock who would

have said this had he my genius ability to twist words: "Life. It's one big ol' egg MacGuffin with cheese."

And I'm alone.

Eating it.

Roll credits.

ROLL CREDITS

Underneath the CREDITS, we view OUTTAKES from various CONFESSIONALS.

CONFESSIONAL - STANLEY

Demonstrates his grandfather's bestiality technique with sheep.

STANLEY

What he would do is grab the sheep by her haunches there and shove them hind legs inside his shit-kickers like that so's the animal don't bolt.

NORM

Shit-kickers. Long rubber boots.

STANLEY

161

Yep. And shove that animal right inside so's she don't move.

NORM

You're certain the animal was a *she*?

STANLEY

Once you've had sheep pussy you'll never date another woman, that's what my granddaddy told me and that's what I believe. To this day.

NORM

That strikes me as true. Your grandfather was a wise man on many levels.

STANLEY

I suppose.

(*short pause*)

But I likes *womens*, that's why I stays away from sheep.

NORM

And play bingo.

STANLEY

Right.

CONFESSIONAL - RUSSELL

NORM

Let's throw out a hypothetical. What if the aliens were to come to you and say, "Russell, the human anus to us is like the British chunnel and it's tourist season. Take me to your sphincter"?

RUSSELL

What if?

NORM

Have you ever seen a UFO?

RUSSELL

Nope, only once in Nevada. Taped it and sent it in to *Sightings*.

NORM

What'd they say?

RUSSELL

They said it wasn't no aliens but the Aurora.

NORM

163

Borealis?

RUSSELL

No. The Aurora is a top secret eyes-only spy plane. Real hush-hush stuff. Scared the tar out of me, by gum!

NORM

How do they know about top secret aircraft though?

RUSSELL

I knew you was gonna ask that.
(*chuckles*)
'Cause they're *Sightings*!

CONFESSIONAL - JESSE

JESSE

How many Black men you got up in this piece?

NORM

Including you, one. And no Black women. But that may change, it all depends on who shows up to bingo.

JESSE

So one Black man and you had to provoke a racial dialogue?

NORM

I didn't mean to offend.

JESSE

You never do! ... But you do. Must be magic the way that works. Here I am keeping it real, talking about foods and my dick and shit, and you gotta bring up race. Make a brotha' mad.

NORM

I feel your anger and I think we should talk about that.

JESSE

(*imitates him*)

I feel your anger. I feel your Black rage. Dance for me, Negro! ... Bitch, suck my dick!

Jesse chucks his ink stamp at the camera.

NORM

That's a costly out-lash if you break the lens.

JESSE

—Make me kill you!

165

He lunges at Norm.

CONFESSIONAL - PULL TABS LADY

NORM
What is your obsession with those pull tab games?

PULL TABS LADY
Pull tabs?

NORM
Yes.

PULL TABS LADY
Pull tabs?

NORM
Yes.

She looks confused.

PULL TAB LADY
Pull—?

NORM

—Okay, thank you very much.

CONFESSIONAL - RUSSELL

NORM

Any last words you'd like to share with the viewing public?

RUSSELL

Anybody who sits and plays bingo for four hours and a half deserves to be anally probed. The Grays know this. So don't be surprised all you bingo lovers if late one night you awaken to a tingling sensation 'cause it might just be aliens.

NORM

—Waiting to tickle your sphincter into epiphany.

RUSSELL

You got it.

EXTERIOR - PICNIC TABLE - DAY

Through a hidden camera we watch the film crew eating sandwiches and laughing. "Boom Mic" Mike keeps quietly to himself.

CAMERA MAN
(*bites a jalapeño popper*)
Craft services is for shit.

PRODUCTION ASSISTANT #1
This movie is for shit.

PRODUCTION ASSISTANT #2
Yeah, Norm's kind of a... well... I don't wanna be mean.

CAMERA MAN
Naw, he's an assclown, you can say it.

PRODUCTION ASSISTANT #2
Think we'll get paid?

CAMERA MAN
You're getting paid? Like he offered you money?

PRODUCTION ASSISTANT #2
No, I'm getting backend.

PRODUCTION ASSISTANT #1
Really? So you get a cut of the Hasbro toy line?

CAMERA MAN

Yeah, little closeted gay Norm dolls. You pull their string
and they wince at the sight of vagina.

PRODUCTION ASSISTANT #2

No, I'm getting paid if this shit makes any money. Which it
won't, so I won't. But at least I get a screen credit.

PRODUCTION ASSISTANT #1

If he spells your name right.

CAMERA MAN

"Boom Mic" Mike: silent man with a deadly plan. What
about you? How'd you land this gig?

"BOOM MIC" MIKE

Norm's my best friend.

They nervously freeze up.

CAMERA MAN

Oh.

FALSE FADE

INTERIOR - STRIP CLUB - NIGHT

Norm interviews LISA LICKER, a stripper who wears a huge crucifix necklace and not much else. She gives Norm a lap dance throughout the interview.

LISA

A documentary?

NORM

Yes.

LISA

This is way freaky.

NORM

So just, any story you've got about Mandy.... It could be an anecdote or.... Anything would be helpful.

LISA

A story? Okay, you're not going to believe this but whatever. I don't care.

NORM

As long as it's true to you. There are no judgments in a
documentary, Lisa. Lisa Licker.

LISA
(*to camera*)
That's just my stage name, folks.
(*laughs*)

NORM
(*also laughs*)
Oh, it's much more than that. Indulge us your tale.

LISA
So anyway, yeah. This is like a couple of months ago. I get
off work, right? And this guy pulls up in a dead. Car. Thingy.

NORM
You mean a hearse?

LISA
Yeah! Wait, you've heard this story!

NORM
(*sighs*)
Oh, *you.*

Norm *boops* her on the nose playfully and shoves a dollar
bill down her g-string.

LISA

Okay, so he pulls up in front of me, right? And he's all, "Do
you believe in God?" And I'm like, Dur! I'm only wearing the
biggest fucking cross ever—Hello!—You know?—Like, who
doesn't? Anyway, I felt like he was testing me, you know?

NORM

Not yet.

Short pause. She waits for him to catch up.

LISA

'Cause he's a vampire!

NORM

(*coughs a laugh*)
Did he have fangs?

LISA

Oh, shit! I left that part out, didn't I? ... Yeah, fangs. Huge.
Like, really big.

172

NORM

Huge.

LISA

And I'm like, "Dude! You file those things down?" And he's
like, "Runs in the family."

NORM

That's creepy.

LISA

No, what's creepy is I turn around and no one else is there.
It was like—

NORM

There were people?

LISA

Yeah. Before. The parking lot was packed.

NORM

And now they're—

LISA

All gone. You don't believe me,
right?—I knew it.

NORM

No—Hey!

LISA

So this guy's like challenging my faith and I start talking
about God, blah-blah, and Jesus and all that. And then he
takes off! He smiles at me like, *Ooh, I'll spare this one*, then,
zoom! Outta there!

NORM

Whelp! Happens! ... So what became of all those other
people who vanished?

Short pause. Lisa stares into the distance as if in a trance.

NORM (CONT'D)

Lisa? ... Lisa Licker?

LISA

(*snaps out of it*)

Huh? Oh. They came back. So tell me something about what
you do.

NORM

But... well, wait. What did the vampire thing have to do with
Mandy?

LISA

I don't know, what?

NORM

No, it's not a riddle.

LISA

I thought you said you wanted a story.

NORM

I did. About Mandy.

LISA

Who's Mandy, anyway? What, you got a thing for her?

NORM

(*a beat; cheerily*)
Okay, thank you for your time!

FADE OUT

HOME THEATER RELEASE
SPECIAL FEATURE

Norm & Mandy Reunited

Jeremy Vaeni is seated alone at a black oval table in front of a backdrop. There are two empty chairs.

JEREMY: Hello, people on the other side of the screen. My name is Jeremy Vaeni and tonight we are all in for a treat because we'll be talking to Norm Plumber about his work, his life, and his feelings on *Free Space: The Real Life Story of a Bingo Queen,* now that he's had quite a few years to reflect. And a little bit later, we'll be talking to the bingo queen herself, Mandy-Alise.

First up, let's get into it here, my friend—I've known this man a long, long time, folks. In fact you may remember him as the man who interviewed me in my book, *I Know Why The Aliens Don't Land!* under the nom deplume, Norm

De Plume... Back from the dead, please welcome, Norm Plumber!

Norm walks on stage left and waves weakly to the camera. He shakes Jeremy's hand and takes the seat to his left closest to him.

JEREMY: Norm, it is great to see you.

NORM: Pretty good to be here.

JEREMY: Just pretty good?

NORM: Well, you did introduce me as 'Back from the dead,' so....

JEREMY: Wow, way to no-sell it. I was referring to the fact that in my book I used this convention of you being a part of my personality that needed to be integrated so that I could be whole.

NORM: That's one way to keep me out of the sequel.

JEREMY: By the way, folks, Norm De Plume as a nom deplume was his idea.

NORM: Witty now as it ever was.

JEREMY: I can't argue the wording of that.

NORM: Where's the audience?

JEREMY: What do you mean?

NORM: Why is there no—I mean it sounds like you're talking to a studio audience, but where are they?

JEREMY: This isn't exactly a spare no expense production, Norm.

NORM: I see.

JEREMY: So how have you been, man? We haven't kept in touch over the years.

NORM: Well that's my doing—

JEREMY: You got the birthday cards?

NORM: No.

JEREMY: They were e-cards. Check your junk mail.

NORM: I don't... that's the point of junk mail, I don't have to check it.

JEREMY: You look good, man, you look good.

NORM: Thanks. I work out.

JEREMY: And the lateral lisp is gone. Tell me how that all went down.

NORM: You saw it in the movie.

JEREMY: But did you check in with a speech pathologist or anything? I mean, like... what... what was their take?

NORM: No.

JEREMY: Oh. So, were you completely psyched to not have to talk like a tween anymore, or—

NORM: I wasn't really psyched about anything that happened during that time. I mean at first I was. I met this girl. Beautiful girl. And then we followed her around, that's cool, you know? Lost my lisp, found myself, uncovered a conspiracy—life was good for a hot second and then I realized that being a dick isn't as freeing as it felt.

JEREMY: And here you're referring to your big revelation. The thing you were keeping from yourself your whole life.

NORM: Yes.

JEREMY: It's not that you were gay....

NORM: No! What? Why would you—?

JEREMY: You were just an angry asshole keeping that bottled up and pretending to be doing good works.

NORM: I love gay people. But no—I mean, yes. Yeah, I was... I thought I was documenting people I would never want to be on my worst day, granted, but it was in a way that might help them move along in their lives and me find myself. In my head, at least, that's how I justified it.

JEREMY: Is that as preposterous to you now coming out of your mouth hole as it is for me hearing it in the ears?

NORM: I... think so? But not as preposterous as what you just said.

JEREMY: Here, let me big picture this for the audience at home. Norm realizes he's doing no good in the world. He's just a troll. And coming to terms with that—not struggling against it but really succumbing to his own worst nature—frees him of the lateral lisp, which is a psychosomatic reminder that he is growth-stunted. But now no longer stunted, he is free. Free of the lisp. Free to be himself.

NORM: —But not free to be myself. See here's the new revelation, and it came a few years later: being an asshole, really owning that and acting it out consciously instead of burying it and pretending not to be? It's all still acting. It's all unfulfilling. It was momentarily freeing to not fake it anymore. But once I got to that point I found myself in new shackles.

JEREMY: The shackles of being an asshole.

NORM: Yeah, the shackles of being a dick.

JEREMY: Like a cock ring.

NORM: Not... no, I don't feel comfortable with that descriptive.

JEREMY: Because you're *not* gay.

NORM: Because it's fucking stupid!

JEREMY: Wow, good to see you too, brother!

NORM: Who are you playing to? Stop playing for laughs when there's no audience.

JEREMY: Camera guy's smiling.

NORM: He doesn't know you.

JEREMY: *You* don't know me—I'm in your junk mail.

NORM: Well... figure it out.

Jeremy holds his right finger to his right ear as if he's outfitted with an earpiece.

JEREMY: Oop! Hold that thought, Norm. I'm being told

we have a very special lady in da hiz-ouse and she's ready to make her way to the stage!

NORM: No one's telling you anything—Are you even wearing an earpiece?

JEREMY: Please welcome to the program... Norm, are you ready?

NORM: I guess.

JEREMY: Nervous?

NORM: No.

JEREMY: You haven't seen this woman in years.

NORM: I saw her in the greenroom before I came out here.

JEREMY: You haven't seen her since you destroyed her life, Norm.

NORM: I saw her... I see her right now. She's standing right there, if you'd just pan the camera.

JEREMY: Please give a warm welcome to Mandy-Alise!

Mandy walks into frame and gives Jeremy a welcoming kiss on the cheek. Norm moves in for the same, but she pats him firmly on the shoulder and takes a seat to his left.

JEREMY: Mandy-Alise, it is gratifying to meet you. Having watched you over and over I feel like I know you.

MANDY: My breasts haven't aged.

JEREMY: There's that.

MANDY: Everything else has.

NORM: You look good.

MANDY: *Good* good? Or *for an aging stripper* good?

NORM: No, I mean it. Look, I'm not that guy anymore.

MANDY: We'll see.

JEREMY: Whoa! Tension city here, folks!

Jeremy pretends to loosen his collar for the audience.

MANDY: I just want everyone to know, there's no audience. And he's doing that.

NORM: See? We're on the same page with that. It's weird, right?

MANDY: It's creepy. I feel like I'm on an infomercial in purgatory—What are they paying this guy?

JEREMY: Speaking of what are they paying... Mandy. Tell us about the success of your board game, Sexecutioner's Noose.

MANDY: I sold the rights to an adult gaming company called Flim Flam Fluck. Like, years ago, and, um... nothing. I dunno. I think they demoed it in Indonesia and the Philippines, but it wasn't a board game. I mean, I dunno what they did with it.

JEREMY: Don't know or don't want to know?

MANDY: I'm told by my legal counsel that I shouldn't say more than that until after the trial.

JEREMY: Whoa! No further questions your honor—Am I right?

MANDY: Is he auditioning for something?

NORM: I dunno for what this is for.

JEREMY: So this is your second big trial, then. After the Smokers Conspiracy, as it was called.

MANDY: I'm really not involved in this one. I was paid for the game. That's all I know. Everything was legal on my end, so....

NORM: That's great. Congratulations. You deserve success.

MANDY: Yeah. Look, the reason I agreed to do this reunion for you is to tell you that all is forgiven, so.... I mean, like, honestly. It's been years. I just... hope you have forgiven yourself or whatever, you know? And—but if not. I forgive you. Because it's bingo. It was a game. I was young. Time to let it go.

JEREMY: Whoa! Mighty big of you, there, Mandy-Alise!

NORM: Well, thank you. I don't know what to say.

MANDY: That's good enough.

JEREMY: So, Mandy, tell us what else has been going on in your life. You got married, right? Tell us about that.

MANDY: I married a wonderful man named Otis.

JEREMY: Seriously?

MANDY: Well, he's my cat. He's needy and cuddly. Smooth sometimes, sometimes cruel, sometimes playful. It's a lot like being married to a man.

JEREMY: Oooooh!

NORM: Please, make it stop.

MANDY: But seriously, not-folks, I *was* married briefly. It didn't take.

NORM: I see what you did there.

JEREMY: Was this back when you were still stripping?

MANDY: Dancing—yes. But I mean, no! I was a pole dance instructor, like the fitness craze, you know? It was at a gym. Totally legit. But I guess it was still too sexy for him to take. Guys are like that. They tell you, 'Oh, I can take it. I don't mind if other guys see you naked as long as you come home to me.' And then they get all needy and freaky.

NORM: Like a cat.

MANDY: Right. But not nearly as cute.

JEREMY: Norm, what's going through your mind right now? Right this second. No pondering, just out with it.

NORM: *Like a cat.*

JEREMY: No, we heard that. After that. What did you think about what Mandy said?

NORM: *Like a cat.* I was still thinking about my observation.

JEREMY: And how is this for you now? Is it a weight off

your chest? How do you feel about being accepted by her as you are?

NORM: That's a really weird question but here's the thing about Mandy: she always accepted me as I was.

JEREMY: Did she see through you?

NORM: Did you?

MANDY: Did I?

NORM: You thought you did.

MANDY: So did you.

NORM: Wait....

MANDY: Think you saw through me, I mean.

NORM: Ah.

JEREMY: Did he?

MANDY: Did you?

NORM: Did I?—Maybe. Yeah. Parts of you. But the rest were my projections. I saw what I wanted to see for better or for worse, but I think that's what most people do. We create an image about a person and then we interact with that like it's them.

JEREMY: Is it?

MANDY: Was it?

NORM: Was I?

JEREMY & MANDY IN UNISON: What?

NORM: Double jinx!

JEREMY: Round of Cokes. Now honestly.... Who did you see when you looked into Mandy's eyes? And was it the same person you saw when you looked into her lowercase l?

MANDY: Gross.

NORM: It was all her.

MANDY: Even the silicone, you asshole.

JEREMY: I'm just the examiner, ma'am. Don't shoot the examiner. He's asking what they're thinking.

MANDY: Which *they*, the people not watching this at home or the invisible studio audience?

NORM: I can answer it. I'll answer it. The truth is I was a sexually frustrated misogynist. When I looked into her eyes I saw God and I saw fire. When I looked at her naked I saw inevitable rejection.

JEREMY: Rejection by God?

NORM: And all that is passion and beauty in this world, yes.

MANDY: Norm, that's so... poetic. God—and sad!

NORM: It *is* sad. I was a miserable man-child pretending to live in a world that was never for me. That's what posers do but it's also just what growing up is about, you know? So I'm not too hard on myself about it.

JEREMY: Let's turn our attention now to the other bingo queen, Ethel. What became of her after the brouhaha died down?

MANDY: Oh, God, Ethel. I haven't thought about that woman in a dog's age.

NORM: She died, didn't she? Shortly after that?

MANDY: No, her nurse did. I think Ethel's now a hundred and two.

NORM: Seriously?

MANDY: No, she's dead.

NORM: I thought so.

MANDY: Not cancer, though. Just old age.

NORM: If it's not one thing it's the other.

MANDY: It's always the other. Waiting for you with a fork and knife at the end of this long table. That's how I picture it. Death drooling and starving like a cartoon.

NORM: In a bib.

MANDY: Definitely wearing a bib.

NORM: Which is weird because he doesn't have anyone to impress. Fuck it. Get a little human mustard on your shirt.

Mandy laughs; Norm and she share a moment.

JEREMY: Whoa! Get a room you two! I'd say this is going swimmingly.

MANDY: Is this a dating show? You're not gonna pull back a curtain and reveal some shitty setup are you, Norm?

NORM: No! Come on! Give me *some* credit here.

JEREMY: It's interesting you asked that, Mandy, because it shows that you care. Does it not?

MANDY: I—

JEREMY: —You're guarded because you care. True or false?

MANDY: No, I care! I do. Norm and I have history. Fucked up and brief but it's there. I have a soft spot for anyone who was in my life just... because they were.

NORM: Now who's the poet?

MANDY: I've got skills. Mad skills.

NORM: Angry skills. Grrr....

JEREMY: Norm? Mandy? Will there be a sequel to *Free Space: The Real Life Story of a Bingo Queen*?

MANDY: Not with me in it, no.

NORM: Never say never, but I've got a lot on my plate as a writer-director. I'm in post on a sci fi movie now called *Clamdemic* and then I go to work on *Fartocalypse*.

MANDY: Never. I'm saying never.

NORM: Sure, you *say* never. But do you *mean* never?

MANDY: It's not ambiguous. It's never.

JEREMY: What is *Clamdemic* about and when can we expect to see it?

NORM: *Clamdemic* tells the story of methane gas rising from the Arctic, hitting red tide during an el niño, creating the perfect storm for mutation. The result is that in the Pacific, clams grow teeth and grow abundant like weeds.

JEREMY: Weeds with teeth.

NORM: Clam weeds with teeth that learn how to propel themselves. And then they learn to feed on human flesh. It's campy.

JEREMY: Crappy?

NORM: No, it'll be great! A campy throwback movie.

JEREMY: Oh, I must have misheard you. I heard *crappy*.

NORM: And you wonder why I never call.

JEREMY: I don't wonder that. When will it be out in theaters?

NORM: *Theaters* might be stretching it a bit. No fixed date but we're shopping it around for a release late next year.

JEREMY: Excellent. And Mandy, what is next in your life? Any big plans you can share with us?

MANDY: Nope. Norm taught me never to make those.

NORM: God, sorry.

MANDY: It is what it is. I'm a stronger person for it.

JEREMY: Should you be thanking him?

MANDY: Oh God, I hate it when people say that! Just because someone fucks you over and you learn from it doesn't make them a teacher. That wasn't their intention.

NORM: It wasn't mine. But I'm glad you grew, if I may say. Growth is good.

JEREMY: Not cancer.

NORM: Christ, is this thing over?

JEREMY: Are you defending cancer?

NORM: Alright, enough. Jeremy, it's been real. Mandy... I'm glad you're okay.

Norm stands, bends down, and gives Mandy a hug where she sits. She is accepting of that.

MANDY: Me, too. I mean you. Glad you're okay.

JEREMY: I'm okay; you're okay. Wasn't there a book called that once?

Mandy looks at Jeremy like he's too pathetic for words.

MANDY: Yeah, I've got to go, too. I think I've found the thing worse than awkward silence and it's awkward loud.

Together, they walk off the set.

NORM: You wanna grab dinner or something?

MANDY: No.

JEREMY: And that will do it, folks! There they go, the director and star of *Free Space: The Real Life Story of a Bingo Queen.* They said this reunion would never happen. Whoever they were they were wrong. It did happen, as you saw, and it was a beautiful thing... that we can fix in post. Somebody call cut before I shit myself—*way* too much coffee today.

He dashes off the set.

AFTERWORDS

That was atrocious. I don't get who's in charge of something like that. There were hair and makeup people. A production assistant flew me out here for this. I'm walking to a car with a driver I will pay with a voucher. But do they screen the questions? Don't they have writers?

Maybe it's chaos theory. Throw spaghetti at the screen and see what sticks. Is that what Spaghetti Westerns were? I don't get it.

"Hey, Mandy! Hold up!"

Norm shouts this through the glass of an automatic revolving door. I turn and watch him try to time his way in with the rush of shuffling executives. He looks like he tumbles out behind them trying to reach me. I keep my smile tight. This is cute, actually.

"You yelled?" I say.

"We meet again," he says. "Coincidence?"

I know he's joking and so am I when I retort, "No, not... nothing about this describes coincidence."

"Listen, sorry about that back there. I don't know what happened."

"It was a bit of an abortion."

"The powers that be thought Jeremy would be good in the role because we go back a long time and he does podcasting."

"I don't know what that is."

"It's an internet radio thing. But listen, I'm doing a B-movie thing and was wondering if you wanted a part in it."

I have acted before. In high school. It wasn't *that* embarrassing. And stripping down to your nothings for drunks takes the wind out of the bashful sail for good. But still... "I dunno know, Norm. *Clam Academy* doesn't really sound like my thing."

"*Clamdemic.*"

"Right."

"No, that's actually finished. I'm talking about *Fartocalypse.*"

I laugh sharply, maybe a little too cruelly but it's not intentional. "That's supposed to win me over, how?"

"I dunno. It's just a fun thing we could do together. It would be absurd. I don't think in the history of cinema a subject from a documentary went on to become the star of the director's sci fi feature. We could make history together."

I mull this for all of one second. "You could just ask

me to a cup of coffee. That's what real humans do."

"They do?"

"Yeah. When they want to do something together. It's not usually, 'Hey, let's change the world!' Or, 'Hey, may I interest you in being a starlet?'"

"It is in LA."

"It isn't in life."

"LA isn't life, that's true. But coffee's so clichéd." He looks at me askance and then asks the askance thing: "Isn't it?"

"Maybe. But it's simple. I'm a simple girl. You need a complicated woman for world-ending flatulence."

"You wouldn't be farting—"

"Or whatever—"

"—The *whole* time. But yeah, I see your point. And I'll raise you a double mocha frappa delta beta kappa, or whatever."

"Alright. Sounds a little pricey. I accept."

"Good. Tomorrow? Pick you up at your hotel? When do you fly out?"

"Couple days. Tomorrow's good. Call me in the morning. Something tells me you've got my number already."

"Good seeing you again."

"Yeah. You too." I say this like I'm admitting it to

myself. I guess I am.

I smile and waggle my fingers at Norm as my driver gets the door for me. So cool being a somebody for a day. Getting the somebody treatment, even if it is for a movie that makes me look like a world class idiot.

Look at Norm standing there. Alone in his head with that sheepish grin as I pull away. I smile and put my hand to the tinted window, but I don't roll it down. He can't see me in here I don't think. It's very mobster. Like a slow-motion getaway.

I lied to Norm just now. I fly out late tonight. Something tells me he knows that, too. I don't feel as guilty about it as I should.

Or should I? I ask myself this askance thing. But I already know the answer.

I want to go home.

ABOUT THE AUTHOR

Jeremy Vaeni is an award-winning writer who has authored *I Know Why the Aliens Don't Land!*, *Urgency.*, and *Into The End*. He is the host of *The Experience*, a weekly podcast in which he interviews experiencers of high strangeness phenomena. This can be heard at: www.unknowncountry.com.

He is also co-host of Paratopia, a podcast that dissects high strangeness phenomena with a depth and clarity beyond anything you've heard. You can hear it now at: www.paratopia.net.

OH, ONE LAST THING

Oh, one last thing. Sooner than you think—like within a few months of publication—I will be releasing the next book in this series, *The Squared Circle*. Perhaps you've heard of it? No? Anyway, it's a dark comedy with thriller-like underpinnings. *Fatal Attraction* thriller, not Michael Jackson's *Thriller*. Anyway again, I bring this up because part of the fun of this B-Movies In A Book Series is that you, the reader, will get to choose what you want to read next.

After the release of *The Squared Circle*, you will have a chance to vote which direction you'd like to go with the third book. Would you rather open the movie screen in your mind's eye to watch one of Norm Plumber's science fiction films, *Clamdemic* or *Fartocalypse*? Or would you rather find out what happened to Hero Gregoropolous in college, which will be a far more riveting choice after you've read *The Squared Circle*?

You'll have the opportunity to vote your interest on

the   B-Movies In A Book Series page at my website:
www.bmoviesinabook.com.

Keep in mind that I will write all of the books eventually, it's simply a matter of which order they get released. So, even if the vote doesn't go your way the book will come out, just not next. Or ever, should I die or lose both my arms and tongue in a horrible accident.

Vote wisely.

Vote often.

Read on!

Free Space   Jeremy Vaeni

Free Space   Jeremy Vaeni